Take the Late Train

Take the Late Train

Jack Messenger

Published 2018 by the Greyhound Press, Nottingham, UK

Cover design: Jack Messenger

Cover photo and greyhound graphic: Pixabay

Author photo: Brigitte Lee Messenger

ISBN 978-0-244-41008-7

For Brigitte and Loulou,
and all those who have lost and won

Reviews are the lifeblood of independent authors. We can never have enough of them, for without reviews there are no sales. Please take time to post a review at your favourite retailer and/or at Goodreads.

You need to spend your time with me,
For love is brief and life is long,
And who knows what we're gonna see,
When the late train rolls along?

Take the Late Train, written by James Ketley
From the album *Audrey Ketley Takes the Late Train*

1

Professor Stephen Ketley sat on the edge of his empty bed and wondered what was wrong with his life. It was a question he asked himself every time he drank a little too much. He groped for an answer, but his stomach hurt. Maybe he wasn't asking the right question.

How much, in fact, had he drunk? Surely a simple calculation: two bottles of red between four people ... plus a glass of champagne before dinner. He and Paul had drunk more than Sarah and Lorna, so ... let's say ... three quarters of a bottle. That was nowhere near enough to worry about his life at – what time is it? – eleven o'clock on a Thursday night – the night of his tenth wedding anniversary.

He sighed and removed his watch. His wallet, he checked, lay inside the bedside drawer, on top of his handkerchiefs. He pulled off his socks and rubbed his feet into the warmth of the carpet. He stretched and yawned.

'It was good tonight, wasn't it?' Sarah spoke over her shoulder, opening the wardrobe, putting away her dress. 'Didn't you think it was good?'

Stephen thought. 'Yes, I did.'

'Lorna was fun, wasn't she?'

'I never knew librarians had such a gay time of it.'

'Don't let her catch you calling her that.'

'Sorry. *Archivist.*' Stephen took off his suit and stood in his shirt and underwear while he pulled at his tie. 'Paul was quiet.'

Sarah, in her robe, searched through a dresser drawer, her head bent low. 'Paul was what?'

'Quiet.' Stephen relished his consonants. *'Sub-dued. Re-ti-cent.'*

Sarah looked thoughtful, walking to the mirror. 'I didn't notice.'

'No? Still ...'

'Hmm?'

'I wonder if everything's all right.'

Sarah, sitting down, tilted her head as she removed an earring. 'With them? Of course it is.'

Stephen watched his wife's auburn hair fall over her shoulder. 'How would you know? Does Lorna tell you things?'

'Now and then. Not lately.'

'Paul never says anything.'

Sarah shrugged. 'Men don't go around telling each other how happy they are.'

Stephen, pyjamas on, went to clean his teeth.

The light in the bathroom, he decided, gave his skin a sallow, unhealthy look. And those blue eyes of his were looking a little bloodshot. He stuck out his tongue. Burgundy red. He gargled with mouthwash. The pain in his stomach ebbed and flowed, settled into a gaseous ache. He put his hand to his abdomen and wondered if he was still losing weight. He'd been pleased to lose a kilo at the age of thirty-seven. Then he'd begun to ask himself if anything was the matter. He'd taken to checking his weight and measuring his calories. When he'd exceeded his daily allowance it still hadn't made a difference. Nothing dramatic, he told himself, as he noted the continuing downward trend, but if it went on for long enough ...

'I'm turning into the Incredible Shrinking Man,' he'd told Sarah one morning, as she headed for the study.

'In what respect?'

'I'm losing weight like nobody's business.'

'That's good.'

He'd looked at his shirtcuffs, the ends of his trousers. 'Do I look shorter to you? Are my clothes too big?'

Sarah had glanced over her shoulder as she opened the door. 'Don't worry. I can always get you a doll's house to live in. Like Grant Williams.'

'Who's Grant Williams?'

'The actor who played the Incredible Shrinking Man.'

Stephen had laughed. 'Is there anything you don't know?'

Sarah had turned, her hand on the doorknob. 'I don't know how to finish writing a book on Die Brücke expressionism. Assuming I do finish it.'

'You'll finish it. You always do.'

Sighing, she had closed the door.

Stephen whiled away the lengthy process of emptying his bladder by wondering about Paul and Lorna. Something hadn't felt right. Something he couldn't put his finger on. Then again, he might have imagined it. He hoped so. He didn't like to think of his friends in trouble.

He flushed the toilet, glancing at the bathroom scales while he washed his hands. Tomorrow, before breakfast.

Sarah was in bed, makeup removed, hair combed out. Her eyes scanned the pages of a big art book about the Matisse chapel in Vence.

Stephen smiled. 'Those reading glasses always make you look terribly forbidding.' He sat in bed, admiring the photographs when his wife turned a page. Her leg felt cold against his. 'Do you know something? This is the first time we've been alone together all day.'

Sarah turned another page, then looked at him over the tops of her spectacles. 'I'm sorry, did you say something?'

'I said this is the first time we've been alone all day.'

'Is it?'

'Just together. Like this. On our own.'

Sarah stared at the darkness beyond the bedroom door. 'Yes. I suppose you're right.'

Stephen admired her sweet little nose. He would lean over and kiss that nose.

Sarah frowned. 'Now you've smudged my glasses.' She turned away, reaching for the cloth in her spectacles case. 'What's the matter? Didn't you have a good time?'

Stephen watched her clean her lenses. 'Oh, yes. It was fun.'

'You don't sound convinced.'

'No, really, it was good.'

Sarah breathed on the smudge and rubbed. 'But?'

Stephen looked at his feet, his toes flexing beneath the quilt. 'But – we have been seeing a lot of people these last few months. I think it would be nice to celebrate our anniversary alone next time. What do you think?'

'I thought we'd decided it would be good to share the occasion.'

'Did we? I don't recall.'

'Yes you do. But if you've changed your mind ...'

'Oh, no. Just as you like.'

Sarah put on her glasses. 'Well, it's up to you. I really don't mind.'

Stephen opened his book and tried to read. 'We have a year to decide.'

Sarah turned a page, revealing a stained glass window in lemon yellow and aquamarine blue. Stephen looked. He admired the innocent light and pure colours. 'I wish I'd chosen art history.'

Sarah raised an eyebrow. 'You've never shown much interest in the subject. Besides, you were made for literature – teaching it, at any rate.'

'I don't know about that. Who reads anymore?'

'Your students, at least.'

'Sometimes I have to prod them awake. Literally. Mind you, I don't blame them. This term feels pretty dull already.'

'It'll be over before you know it.'

Stephen nodded. 'Then Christmas. And New Year.' He glanced at his wife. 'We'll have to see my mother.'

Sarah turned another page. 'I should really go and visit this place. I feel a fraud every time I tell my students about it.'

'Next summer, perhaps.'

'Why next summer?'

'The light.'

Sarah nodded, scratching her leg beneath the quilt. 'At your mother's house?'

'That would be best.'

'We could go for the day, I suppose.'

'I was thinking of a weekend. Or perhaps longer.'

Sarah looked up. 'I can't. I really have to concentrate on my book. The deadline's close and there's still a lot to write.'

Stephen frowned. 'What do you suggest?'

'We could go up to see your mother, then you could stay over while I come straight home. Then, when you got back, we could have New Year together.'

'What about Emma?'

'Emma?'

'Your daughter.'

'I *meant* what about her?'

'Will she spend Christmas with her father or with us?'

Sarah shrugged. 'I hope she'll stay with Andrew. My book – '

'Are Paul and Lorna giving their usual New Year's party?'

'Yes. There's that, of course.'

Stephen nodded, considered. 'My mother will be hurt to see you leave.'

Sarah laughed. 'Audrey *hurt*? She'll be delighted! You're her boy, after all. I count as much as Angela.'

Stephen frowned, slipped a hand to his aching stomach. 'She never has a bad word to say about you.'

'She doesn't have to, you know that. Those conversational tics of hers ...'

'What do you mean?'

'Oh, the way she talks! A little inflection here, a pause there, and you're condemned for life. No thank you!'

'Sarah – '

'No wonder Angela's the way she is.'

Stephen smiled. 'You hardly know Angela.'

'I don't have to know her. She got out when she could, so good for her. I would have done the same. It's no fun living with a drunk.'

Stephen drew back. The truth about Audrey always hurt when it came from someone else. Angela had shouted those same words many times, over many years. 'She's unhappy.'

'Who's unhappy?'

'My sister.'

'*You* hardly know her. Besides, just because she lives the life she has it doesn't mean she's unhappy. You mustn't imagine yourself in her place.'

Sarah read, turned another page.

Outside, someone walked by, a laugh echoing to silence. Stephen found it irritating, that sound of a stranger's pleasure. The annoyance mingled with the pain in his belly. He opened his book and began to read, his mind wandering to his mother, his sister, the Gillespies. And Christmas. He glanced at his wife. She was gazing at the open door. 'Tired?'

Sarah lifted a hand to her mouth. 'Yes. I need to sleep. Mind if I turn off the light?'

'No. I'm tired, too.'

'Goodnight.'

'Goodnight, Sweetheart. Happy anniversary.'

Stephen lay in the dark and listened to the sound of their breathing. The pain in his belly eased. He reached for Sarah's hand, resting his palm over her small knuckles and slender fingers. He tried to recall the last time they had made love. 'Sarah? Are you awake?'

His wife inhaled.

'I hope we don't turn into one of those couples who have so many things it's important not to talk about.'

Exhaled.

Stephen turned over, searched for comfort. 'Perhaps we already are.'

Later, he felt again for Sarah's hand and clutched at emptiness. He must have been dreaming. He turned and looked at the ceiling. A grey light filtered through the curtains and sketched the room in shades of night. The air, cold against his face, chilled his dream. Something to do with the Gillespies. Somebody had said something unpleasant.

Stephen yawned. A stupid dream. He switched on the lamp, his feet finding his slippers. He shivered in his dressing gown, walking to the bathroom. Empty. At the top of the stairs he looked down into darkness. 'Sarah?'

In the hall there was light beneath the study door. He knocked, coughed, went in. His wife looked up, frowned. 'Did I wake you?'

'I wondered where you were. What are you doing?'

'I couldn't sleep so I came down to work.'

'You know that's not a good idea. You won't accomplish much at this hour.'

'What time is it?'

'I don't know. Late – or early. Come to bed.'

'I will in a minute. You go back to sleep.'

Stephen yawned. 'Would you like something to drink?'

'No. You go to bed.'

He watched her working. 'You certainly look tired. Why can't you sleep?'

'Oh, I don't know! Please don't ask me questions now. I'm too tired to respond.'

'Then you must be too tired to work.' Stephen approached her desk. Sarah shuffled some papers and put them away. His arm around her shoulders, he crouched awkwardly, his face against hers. 'Do you know what I wish?'

'No. Surprise me.'

'I wish you'd never started this damn book. I can't remember a time when you haven't been writing it.'

'Remember all the times I said the same thing to you?' Sarah patted his cheek. 'It will be over soon. As long as I can put in the hours before the new year.'

'I just don't like to see you shut yourself away night after night. Next time, write something short and sweet.'

Sarah jammed on her glasses. 'There's not going to be a next time for some while, believe me.'

Stephen shivered, headed for the door. 'Ever since you started this thing it feels like we're either with a lot of other people or locked away in our own rooms. That's why I was hoping this Christmas we could be together.'

'We will be together. I don't intend to work all the time, you know. Now, you go to bed. I'll be up in a while.'

Stephen lay awake until Sarah returned. He curled himself behind her, wrapped his arm around her waist. Her soft hair with its familiar aroma soothed his tiredness. He fell asleep amid confused images of his mother and sister, the voices at dinner babbling in his ear.

In the morning, he awoke to a headache that hammered at his skull while Sarah showered. They rushed through breakfast. At the front door, Stephen glanced at her as she rummaged through her overstuffed satchel. 'Will you be free for lunch?'

'That would be nice. No, wait. I'm sorry, I can't. I have an arts faculty meeting.'

'Pity.'

'You're visiting Audrey tomorrow, aren't you? Where the hell's my hairbrush?'

'Am I?'

'You were thinking about it. Or Sunday.'

'I don't know. Perhaps tomorrow.'

The hairbrush was found. 'Do you want to ask Emma if she's free? She likes you at the moment. And Audrey. Besides, we haven't been getting on well lately. She'll enjoy the day out.'

'Do you want to come?'

'Good God no. I really must continue writing. Every weekend counts. Besides, I don't see –'

'But you know how things are. Ever since Dad died, Mother's been living alone in that big house with no one around. She only has Mrs MacDougall for company two days a week. I have to go and see her now and then.'

'I know you do. Now and then. Not all the bloody time.'

'It's not far, after all.'

'You don't have to convince me.'

Stephen looked at his feet. 'I suppose one day we'll have to make a decision about her future.'

Sarah put on her coat. 'You know what will happen as well as I do. All the work will devolve onto you. Angela won't help.'

'No. I can't accuse my sister of making the most of her family or her life.'

'Can anyone really know?'

Stephen pursed his lips. 'Isn't it obvious? Last I heard, she was involved with some musician or other with little concept of monogamy. Buzz – if that really is his name – spends his time wandering between folk festivals and other women, as far as I can make out. Angela doesn't encourage questions. I don't think we've really talked for years. I can't even remember the last time we met.'

Sarah flicked her hair over her collar and checked the mirror, brush at the ready. 'I don't understand all this latent hostility in your family. It's like something out of Harold Pinter.'

Stephen looked on as she neatened her hair. 'Angela always refused to help herself. She never thought about anything, that was her trouble. Just one crisis after another, until everyone around her got sick of it and saw that nothing could be done. It makes me angry.'

'Why should you be angry?'

'It's such a waste. She really could have made something of herself.' Stephen frowned, calmed himself. He was beginning to sound like his father.

Sarah sniffed and walked to the door. 'Anyway, it's nothing to do with me. See you this evening.'

They kissed goodbye, their eyes averted.

Stephen caught the campus bus and watched the Christmas

streets floating past. Ten years married. All those days and nights. The time had dropped behind him like a half-remembered dream. The bus lurched at a roundabout, his head striking the window. He ran a hand through his hair. Tomorrow, he should take the train to see Audrey. On her own with too much time to drink – it wasn't good.

George Ringer came to see him in his office on the third floor. 'Have you heard?'

Stephen began to empty his bag. 'Morning, George. Heard what?'

'Noah Tredwell's wife has left him. They'll have to change his biography. It says – here, let me.'

George reached inside Stephen's bag and pulled out the book Stephen had barely begun to read. He looked past the delirious reviews and read that the author and his wife, Ann, lived happily in Nottingham on the banks of the Trent. George seemed delighted by the news. 'I always thought there was something wrong there.'

'I wouldn't know.' Stephen tugged at the loose waistband of his trousers and remembered he'd forgotten to weigh himself. 'Do I look smaller to you?'

'Smaller?'

'Thinner.'

George scrutinized him, his face bland. 'Possibly. Does it

matter?'

'I don't know.'

George shrugged, carried on. 'I know – knew – Ann slightly. She worked over on the other campus. Postcolonial studies.'

'Specializing in postmarital trauma?'

George laughed.

'I thought he was ill,' said Stephen.

'Some mental problem. Evidently too much for the wife.'

Stephen dropped a stack of essays onto his desk. 'Well, thanks for telling me this, George. I'll try to think of dazzling new insights for my class on the contemporary novel this morning.'

'Take it as a warning, Stephen.'

'A warning? About what?' Stephen, puzzled, looked at George, who seemed more than ever like an elongated, somewhat flabby Mr Pickwick, his chestnut hair unkempt, his brown eyes the colour of Nottingham Best Bitter.

George peered at him over his hornrims. 'If you must put Tredwell's novels on your reading list ... '

'We're not going to go through that again, are we?'

George smiled, strolled to the window, hands in his pockets. He removed his glasses, peered earthward. 'Car parks are fascinating places.'

Stephen turned on his computer. 'Just as well, given the view.'

'All human life is here ... even Gordon Zellaby. Forgotten his bag again ... now he's forgotten to lock his car. What's got into him?'

'Our glorious leader has higher things on his mind.'

George scanned the comings and goings. 'A lot of these students drive better motors than mine. Have you noticed?'

'Everyone drives a better motor than yours. Except me. I don't have a motor.'

'Good Lord! Look at that Jag! How do the bastards manage it, I wonder?'

'They feel flush from all those loans. They'll suffer for it in the end.'

'I hope so. Doesn't seem fair somehow.'

'Your cordial detestation of the young men and women who keep you in gainful employment has always amused me, George.'

'I detest everyone, not just my students. Faculty. Everyone. Especially faculty.' George looked over his shoulder. 'Of course, I don't include you in that, Stephen. You are the one colleague here for whom hope remains alive.'

'I'm glad to hear it.'

'You have not allowed yourself to be ground down by the relentless march of progress. The conversion of this once noble institute of higher learning into a diploma supermarket has not perturbed you in the slightest.'

Stephen watched his emails arriving. 'If the student is willing to pay ... '

'Then they must damn well have some kind of qualification to show for it, no matter how worthless. "Can't spell? Unable to read? No problem! Give us a hundred thousand forints and this charmingly designed certificate of attendance will be yours. Now you too can boast of having studied at this financially secure and morally bankrupt university."'

'I suspect you're becoming disillusioned, George.'

George laughed, without humour. 'I'll tell you a secret, my boy. The thrill has gone, but it's really gone.'

Stephen looked up. 'Is it that bad?'

George nodded, scratched his forehead. 'It's like a marriage. Once the sex goes, everything goes.'

'You've never been married.'

'A mere detail, Stephen! Believe me, I know. Look at the Tredwells.'

'How can you possibly know about the Tredwells?'

George whispered lasciviously. 'Rumours abound that the luscious Ann was taking her charms to breakfast elsewhere.'

'I don't want to know.'

'And speaking of luscious charms – '

'Sarah is well, thank you, and we had breakfast together this morning, as usual.'

George chuckled and checked his watch. 'Good God! You've

kept me here way beyond my time, Stephen. I do wish you'd learn to control your insatiable appetite for gossip.'

George gone, Stephen paused, walked to the window. The sky wore a coat of grey cloud. Human breath and vehicle exhaust fumes drifted through the car park. An aircraft rumbled somewhere far off. He thought about the Tredwells, the Gillespies. Perhaps he should talk to Paul. Tomorrow? No, that was out. He would catch the train to see his mother. These dull days of autumn would be getting her down.

Disillusionment, he had read often enough, can easily set in around the age of forty – look at George. George really hated teaching, had hated it for years, as he had hated his students and hated his institution, as long as Stephen could remember. Stephen liked teaching. He liked it now as he strode towards his first class of the day.

Zellaby stepped out of his office and stalked down the corridor. 'Morning, Gordon.'

'Hmm? Oh ... Morning, uh ... Morning!'

Stephen frowned, wondered if he'd done something wrong, thought not. He stopped by the lavatories and looked at himself in the mirror. He was definitely looking a little – reduced. His cheeks seemed sunken – that was new. He puffed them out, stood in profile, appalled at his thinness.

Then, combing his hair, he heard someone weeping in one of

the cubicles. For a moment he wondered if it was George, desperate before another dismal day of work, but weeping wasn't George's style. George was too sarcastic for tears.

Stephen pocketed his comb, unable to ignore all that human anguish. It was a lonely, helpless sound – inconsolable. His own face looked at him, suddenly bleak and bereft. His eyes were moist and he wondered why. He'd felt all right until this minute. Now, it was like hearing himself on the other side of midnight.

He glanced at the cubicle, bit his lip. Should he say something? It wasn't as if he could knock. He should mind his own business. Anyway, it was time for his class.

'Good morning, everyone.'

Stephen sat down and took out the notes he knew he didn't need but which gave him something to do with his hands. 'Right. Where were we?'

'English literatures beyond the metropole; English languages rather than the English language.'

'Thank you, Jenny.'

Stephen had a gift for teaching, everybody said so. He'd remembered all the dull and boring teachers he'd encountered over the years, who had made many of humanity's greatest achievements sound trite and insipid. He could still recall their monotonous voices droning on and on, their contempt for themselves and their sullen students. Maybe George was like that.

Then there had been the good, the inspiring communicators, full of enthusiasm and excitement, eager to learn. That was something Stephen had realized from the beginning: the importance of mutual discovery. You couldn't pour knowledge into another person's brain, but you could enable them to think and find out for themselves.

In his office at the end of the morning, he scanned the stacks of essays and correspondence arranged for his attention. Another twenty-six emails had arrived since 9 a.m. He picked up his paper knife. There was a knock at the door.

'Come in!'

Stephen looked up and failed to recognize the young man in jeans and t-shirt. His brown hair was cut short and he hadn't shaved. Only his eyes – green, deep and restless – were remarkable. They looked everywhere except straight ahead.

'Professor Ketley?'

Stephen put a name to the face. Jack Caswell. A first-year student who spent his time at the back of the room, contributing nothing, leaving as soon as he could. The one essay he'd been obliged to write was mediocre.

'Please sit down, Jack. When people stand in front of me like that it makes me feel nervous.'

Jack glanced at him, Stephen indicating the vacant chair.

'Now, what's on your mind?'

‘Professor Ketley, I shouldn’t be here. I don’t belong.’

2

Emma – sixteen years old, long straight hair as brown as her eyes – sat opposite Stephen, head bowed, her thumb poised over her mobile. A minute before departure.

'Civil engineering?'

Emma laughed, brushed her fringe across her forehead. 'I knew you wouldn't approve.'

'Approve? I'm delighted! It's a great thought.'

Emma looked pleased.

'Besides, does it really matter what I think?'

'No, I suppose not. But it helps.'

'Cambridge, too! Top of the rankings. I checked.' The automatic doors ground shut; the train lurched and roared. 'We're off.'

Emma became engrossed in texting. Stephen watched, fascinated by her dexterity. Nottingham station slipped away, his mother waiting at the other end of an hour.

Emma looked up. 'Has Mum said anything?'

Stephen tried to recall. He saw his wife's back disappearing behind the study door. 'Oh, she'll be pleased.' Emma looked dubious, so he added: 'I can tell. You know how Sarah is. But she'll be very excited.'

Emma seemed convinced. She looked out the window, half-smiling.

'How about your father? What does he say?'

'He'll be glad if I follow in his footsteps. Especially if it means I can help him out during vacations.'

'The practical experience he can give you would be invaluable – really give you an advantage.'

Emma nodded, watched the countryside go by.

'How are things between you both?'

She shrugged, pulled a face. 'All right. We have our moments.'

'Like with your mother?'

'A bit. It's hard to shuttle between the two of them. They always make me feel I've betrayed them?'

'One day soon you'll be your own person and things will settle down. In the meantime, at least you have two homes you can call your own. And when you're a civil engineer you can build another.'

Emma smiled. 'Like ... '

Stephen laughed. 'Like what?'

'Like, I thought, you might be disappointed?'

'I can't imagine you ever disappointing me, Emma, or your parents.'

'But it's not English literature or art.'

Stephen shrugged. 'So what? Most art is pretty pathetic, after all.' He sighed, scratched his head. 'When I was your age everyone looked down on anyone who could do things. Now I'm older, I regret not being practical. It's difficult to feel useful when what you do has no obvious value. Not like bridges and buildings. If you can find ways of working on ecological stuff then you'd really be helping the world.'

Emma nodded. 'That's what I thought.'

'Good for you.'

Stephen smiled. Emma's company was agreeable, the journey pleasant.

He watched as the railway joined the slopes above the Derwent. Next stop, Ambergate. He knew them all by heart, each little painted station: Ambergate–Whatstandwell–Cromford–Matlock Bath–Matlock. The train wound through the wooded valleys and bare hillsides, crossed the gentle river fretted over with branches, clogged with fallen leaves. The sun appeared, burning away the mist, sending warmth through the frosted window.

Emma spoke. 'Of course, I'll always love reading.'

'I should hope so.'

'And music and art. But I thought: what's really important? Like, the world's a mess and getting worse. We have to find ways to ... build a sustainable future. You know?'

'Yes, I know.'

Emma's face reddened. 'I didn't mean to criticize your choices.'

'Don't worry.'

Emma's phone expressed panic. 'Excuse me.'

Stephen watched her find a space alone. The carriage shuddered over a crossing, drowning her urgent whispers. He wondered who it was on the other end of that teenage lifeline. That she was free to join him for the day had surprised him. Perhaps she was running away from some unhappy situation. Another bust-up with her father, or a friend or lover.

Do girls her age have lovers?

Best not to think about it. Too dangerous, too tired.

Sleep.

Do girls her age have lovers?

Sleep!

Fifteen years ago, hot on the trail of Edith Wharton and a PhD, Stephen journeys to Florence for a summer of study. He works hard and learns Italian. He enjoys his youth for the first time, it seems to him, away from his parents and their mutual self-destruction.

He meets Giuliana. She invites her friends to her parents' villa high in the hills above Florence, where all is calm and beauty, a casual elegance of the neglected kind. Stephen talks and drinks and dreams of the future while Giuliana listens. He has plans – half-formed, confused. And he tells her he wants to write. He has things to say, stories to tell. But, of course, so many things are also important ... And he listens to her as she tells him of her life, so strange and new. He wonders at her silences, the faint suggestion of expectation in her smile and averted eyes, until one evening they kiss and find heaven. She dismisses her friends so that the two of them can be alone and watch the sunsets undisturbed by foolish chatter. Days of study and nights of passion, meals *al fresco*, long walks in the cool of the evening, until it is time for him to leave.

His last day with her on the terrace overlooking the city. Sitting in the shade of trees whose names he will never learn, they hold hands with quiet desperation. He tells her he will miss her. She remains silent. He says he will return. She looks at him and says, 'I wonder if you will. I don't think you know.' He tries to convince her, but his words are broken, ineffectual, make her laugh. 'You must go home and decide what you really want,' she tells him. 'There is life and there is living. We all know what we want as soon as we learn we've lost it.'

Now, here in this carriage with his wife's daughter by another man, he tries to remember what it was Giuliana meant, all those years ago.

'Stephen?'

'Hmm?'

'Matlock. Come on! We're here.'

They climbed the hill to Audrey's house, hidden behind the leafless trees draping the valley. Behind them, the noise of the town, the faint rush of the river. The sky was tinged with blue, the clouds a crumbling phalanx.

They stopped to catch their breath, Stephen's heart racing. 'I'm glad you could come, Emma. You can carry me the rest of the way.'

Emma blushed. 'How long is it since you've been here?'

'Oh – weeks. A month. I don't know what state she'll be in. Try not to be shocked by anything.'

'I like Audrey. Why would I be shocked?'

Stephen heard music tumbling from an upstairs window. He wiped his forehead with his sleeve, and checked his watch. 'She's started early today.'

'What's that tune?'

The music – insistent, too faint to catch – beat beneath their footsteps. 'A ballad. A slow one. Audrey always preferred the standards. She liked to improvise.'

They walked some more, then Emma stopped.

Stephen looked back. 'Don't tell me you're tired as well?'

'No. It's just that ... well ... I wanted to ask you something?'

'What is it?'

Emma looked up at the trees, fidgeted with her mobile. 'I'm thinking of taking a year off.'

'Oh?'

She spoke quickly. 'I think it would do me good. Work as a barista or something? Just to make sure I really want to carry on with studying?' She waited for his reaction.

Stephen gulped at the frozen air, stalled for time. 'Ah! A secret plan?'

'Kind of.'

'So what is it you want to ask?'

'Could you break the news to Mum? You know ... break it gently?'

Stephen, sighing, put his arm through Emma's and led her slowly up the hill. Her perfume, young and insistent, raged over him. 'It's fine to take a year off, Emma. You'll find out about the wonderful world of work, which can be pretty harsh, I'm afraid. But, do you think it's the right time to do it? What I mean is, why not carry on till university and then see?'

'I want to do it now.'

'Are there any complications that worry you? Close friends you'll miss?' Stephen swallowed. 'A boyfriend?'

Emma shook her head. 'Nothing like that. It's ... well, when I see Mum I wonder if that's the kind of life I really want.'

'Civil engineering is nothing like what she does.'

'I know it. But years and years of study ... I'm not sure I have it in me.'

'I think you have. So does Sarah. You've certainly got the brains.'

At the open gate with its unruly hedge and rough gravel drive, they turned to admire the view. Matlock, grey and purposeful, went about its business. They could see the gardens along by the river, bare and brown. Dogs barked at a flock of wheeling rooks. Further down the line, the rumble and rush of an approaching train. The air felt bright and chill, thick with the aromas of dank forest and woodsmoke.

'So, will you tell her?'

'If that's what you really want. I'm just concerned you don't make a mistake like ... that you don't throw away something before you know what you have.'

Audrey must have changed the record. A silence he hadn't noticed was filled abruptly by sombre piano. Then his mother's voice. He strained to catch the words.

And yet it's dreadfully near ...

'Angel Heart.' Stephen looked at Emma, who stared at the ground, intent. He admired her prettiness in that awkward stepfatherly way to which they'd adapted and made their own, shy with one another yet strangely intimate. They had found shelter together from Andrew and Sarah, from Audrey, but soon she would no longer need him. Emma was virtually a woman now, he realized, and it felt like the first time he'd noticed.

My anxious heart won't hear the sound ...

The lyrics echoed strangely, as if held in the house beyond their time. Stephen recognized the recording. Live at Ronnie Scott's, Audrey on the same bill as Blossom Dearie.

The old stones – covered now with a slick of rain-soaked leaves – crunched beneath their shoes. The Victorian house disclosed itself beyond a holly bush he'd fallen into one summer as a child, clad in shorts and bare feet. He admired the green leaves flushed pink at their crinkled edge, holding no grudge.

The same doubtful roof still held after another year, the stone tiles glistening, the bristling chimneys tall and assertive. The windows were shuttered on the first floor, save for his mother's room. The window there was open as usual, as Audrey believed in the virtues of fresh air, and escaping music.

A brief intro, then Lullaby of Birdland fluttered over Stephen's upturned face. He began to speak, but Emma said 'Hush!' and they listened to the song, wondering at his mother's voice, at all that joy and discipline wrapped up for people's delight. Applause cascaded over the garden.

'Encore!' shouted Emma. 'Encore!'

'Mother!' Stephen repeated the shout, feeling like a little boy lost until he saw Audrey's face at the open window.

'Stephen! And Emma! My dears! Come up! I'm here with Ella and Billie! They've hurt themselves!'

The greyhounds lay curled in the tangled quilt on his mother's bed. Ella had a bandaged hind paw, Billie a nasty scrape on her front leg. They looked at their visitors, eyes bright and sad.

'What happened?' Stephen sat down on the bed and held their heads.

'Billie fell over chasing a duck by the river and Ella trod on some glass. Those bastard yobs who smash their bottles as soon as they've finished drinking! They make me sick! They're both on antibiotics and Ella needed an operation. A thousand pounds, can you believe it? Just for two bloody stitches!'

His mother sat beside him, patting her son and her dogs. She smelled of patchouli and alcohol. Her dress was all frills, her beads and bangles rattling chaos. She looked at Emma. 'How's your mother?'

'She's fine. She sends her love. She's sorry she couldn't come today.'

'I'm sure she must be very busy.' Audrey sniffed, a brave smile sending shock waves over her powdered face.

'She has a book to finish,' Stephen explained.

'Still? Or is this another one?'

'The same, I think.'

Audrey looked dubious. 'Must be some book.' She scrutinized

him. 'Are you eating enough? You look thin to me. Stand up.'

Stephen stood up. 'I have lost – '

'There's nothing left of you!' Audrey wedged her fingers into his waistband, pulled and shook at his trousers. 'If you're too busy to eat then you're too busy is what I say. We'll have to have a big lunch.'

'Here?'

'No. We'll go out. Just the three of us.'

Stephen made coffee and brought it to the sitting room. He opened the shutters and saw the garden sloping to the trees beyond the wall, the greenhouse tucked behind a couple of potting sheds, their doors swinging in the breeze. The grass had been left too late before the autumn rains. It would be hell to mow next spring. 'Do you still have help with all this?'

'They saw to the trees a while ago. The lawn they neglected. Someone was ill, apparently.'

'I'm glad Dad isn't here to see it now.'

'If he were here to see it now it wouldn't look like this. Still, we were up to our necks in produce. You should have seen the apples, Stephen! Just like when you were a boy. Remember?'

'What did you do with them all?'

'Mrs MacDougall froze a lot of puddings. And people come running when there's stuff on offer.'

'Did you give them a concert?' asked Emma. 'We could hear

the music from the railway station, couldn't we, Stephen?'

Stephen frowned.

Audrey looked delighted. 'Does it really carry that far?'

Billie, all silk and gold, padded in and sniffed at Emma's shoes. Ella scrambled down the stairs, her bandaged paw shushing over the quarry tiles in the hall.

'Ella! You know you're supposed to keep off that foot.' Audrey pulled a cushion from the sofa and put it at her feet. Ella turned circles, lay down, watched Stephen.

'How is Mrs MacDougall?' asked Stephen.

'Strong as an ox. You just missed her.'

'Oh? Saturday isn't her day, is it?'

'She drops by now and then, to chat.'

'Well beyond the call of duty, I'd say.'

'What on earth do you mean? We're very good friends. In our way. She tells me everything that's going on in town, otherwise I'd hear nothing.'

'What about your cronies? You still see them.'

'Don't call them that!'

'That's what they are. Cardsharps and drinking companions. Hungry for men.'

Audrey laughed, looked at Emma, pleased. 'Is that how you think of me?'

Emma smiled. 'That's how everyone thinks of you. You have a

reputation.'

'It's only because I sang in nightclubs. Right away people think you're running with gangsters and dating film stars.'

'In your case, it's true. At least, that's what you told me.'

'Did I? Oh, well, for a while there it was true. I had my looks then.'

'What did you look like, Audrey?' asked Emma. 'I can't tell from your psychedelic album covers.'

Audrey struggled to her feet, her chin held high, eyes wide and shining, hands pressed to her thighs. 'I wish you could have seen me, Emma! I was really something! Everyone said so.' She raised an arm, as if she were about to change a light bulb. 'On stage I was one of the best. Just a single spot, right on my face. That's all you could see of me, at first. I always wore black. A slinky black dress they used to call a barbed-wire number.'

'Why?'

'It protected the territory without spoiling the view.'

Audrey laughed her hysterical drink-soaked laugh. Emma joined in. Stephen crossed his legs.

She leaned confidentially towards Emma. 'My hair was dark as well – short, beautifully styled – geometric, you know – like they did then and don't know how anymore.' She sighed. 'Oh well!' Sitting back against the cushions, one hand on Billie's ears, she looked down at her sagging bodice. 'I was really stacked in those days.'

'Mother ... '

'Hard to believe now, but they always said with that voice and those tits nothing could stop me.'

'Mother!'

'Mother what?'

'We don't want to know!'

Audrey scowled her impatience. 'Why are people your generation such bloody prudes? When you were a baby you couldn't get enough of them.' She turned to Emma. 'Of course, if a woman had talent she could look like the back end of a bus and still make it. Look at Ella.' Ella lifted her head. 'Not you dear! Ms Fitzgerald.'

Emma laughed again. 'So what happened?'

Audrey turned her head. 'Happened? Oh, well, then I met Stephen's father.'

'Why did you marry him and not someone else?'

Stephen looked at Emma.

Audrey, oblivious, immediately wistful, cradled her coffee cup. 'Love and necessity, I suppose you'd call it. Jim was wonderful in those days. A great talent. They still sing his songs, you know – No Heart for Loving and While Away the Loneliness are part of the repertoire now. When we met, he looked so cool and good looking – and he was hung like a horse.'

'Mother! For God's sake!'

Audrey stuck out her tongue. 'He'd write songs for me to sing and I'd sing them thinking of him. That was when I had a voice. Then Stephen got going and we decided we'd make it legal.'

'What about your career?'

Audrey was in one of her honest moods. She shrugged, tilted her head. 'That was over with before it really ever began. "Promise unfulfilled" is what they called it. A decade of triumph. A few great records. And then ... ' Audrey gestured with an empty hand, looked at her son. 'I had three big accidents in my life, Stephen: you, your father, and Angela. In that order.'

Stephen was surprised. 'Angela, too?'

'Your father insisted I keep her. So I did. With subsequent effects on career and happiness.'

'Don't let's start on that again. You know it isn't true.'

'It's true all right. If it hadn't been for her I'd be singing now.'

'You might as well blame Dad while you're at it.'

'I do.'

'After all ... '

Audrey glanced at the drinks cabinet, fidgeted with her necklaces. Stephen followed the glance and saw two empty glasses. She and Mrs MacDougall this morning.

Emma came to sit at Audrey's feet and stroke Ella. 'Have you heard from Angela?'

Audrey waved a dismissive hand, her bangles clattering. 'Not a peep. She still with that idiot loafer – what's his name? Bing?'

Stephen sighed. 'Buzz. I think so. I don't know.'

'Your sister was nothing but trouble from the day she was born – conceived. What a waste of a life! She never could hold to anything.'

'Yet, when I remember her as a child ...'

'Who'd have thought a daughter of mine would end up as a dry cleaner. It's embarrassing.'

'There's nothing wrong with dry cleaning.'

'Don't try to defend her, Stephen. I've made allowances, you can't say I haven't, but facts have to be faced. Your father saw that straight away. He could see you were going places. Angela was a great disappointment to him.'

Stephen waited in the garden while Audrey dressed for lunch. The sun shone from behind a haze of cloud, warming the breeze. A gentle autumn morning. He fastened the shed doors and checked the greenhouse for broken glass. The fruit trees were bare and brittle, the grass worn away beneath the branches, studded with rotting windfalls. The valley drew life from the sun, light glinting off rippling water and speeding chrome.

So Angela had also been an accident. A charming way to put it – accident. How casually these squalid little secrets come tripping off her tongue. The nearest she gets to scatting these days. Were there any more of them? Stephen wondered if his sister knew. He'd known about himself for years. In one way or another, he'd never been allowed to forget.

He walked to a column of light squeezed between a tattered hedge.

A deep breath of warm air, his eyes closed.

A childhood memory assails him, pungent, alive. He stands and wonders at it.

Stephen aged eleven is playing hide-and-seek with his sister aged seven. In that big green garden overlooking the Matlock valley, surrounded by wooded hills, and with a view of the river through the branches of the old oaks near the back wall, they have any number of places to hide. Their games are long and intense. He looks everywhere for Angela. She's not inside either of the two sheds. He looks anyway, although he knows she's afraid of the dark. The greenhouse next to the vegetable garden offers no concealment, so he pokes about the trees and hedges along the boundary of the garden before trying the garage and the outside toilet that still works. He is standing on the grass beneath the apple trees, wondering what to do, when his father calls him. He runs inside the house and forgets his sister and their game.

What it is that his father wants him to learn or do or observe Stephen can no longer recall, but he can see the two of them bent over something on the dining table, their eyes fixed on a map spread open ... yes, a walk, that's it. They're always planning walks and reading maps for every last piece of information, as maps and walks provide innumerable opportunities for learning and discovery. And Stephen has become lost in contemplation and planning, his father's pipe tobacco enfolding them in a warm aroma of port wine and cinnamon.

And then Angela walks in with a look of fury and tears in her eyes. Her arms are scratched to bleeding and she holds her hands where they've been stung in a bed of nettles. She's been hiding God knows where for what seems hours, and been forgotten. 'You're horrible, horrible, horrible!' Stephen turns red with shame, but his father looks at Angela with derision. 'Girl, don't be so stupid.'

'Stephen! Taxi's here. Stephen!'

He took a deep breath and felt his waistband slip another fraction. He hitched it up, walking back over the wet grass, his limbs heavy. Through the windows he could see Audrey in the sitting room. He watched her move about, no doubt humming some tune or other, while she picked up a scarf from the sofa, then checked herself in the mirror above the fireplace. He saw her hesitate at the door, then head for the drinks cabinet, her head snapping back when she took a belt of something straight from the bottle.

Emma was waiting when he turned the corner of the house.

'Why did you pull that face a while ago? You looked disapproving.'

Stephen, irritated, tried to be gentle. 'It's just that I avoid talking about certain subjects with Audrey. They upset her. She's on her own now, and it does her no good living in the past. Please don't encourage her.'

'I think she likes to talk. She wasn't upset.'

'It's just a little ... tactless to ask certain questions.'

Emma frowned her incomprehension. 'What questions?'

'About my father, about her career.'

'But she's always going on about her career! It's what she enjoys. You heard the music.'

Stephen lost his temper. 'Emma, please allow me to be the best judge of what is and isn't good for my own mother, okay?'

Emma, turning away, ran to the greyhounds sniffing at the taxi driver through the car window. Stephen bit his lip. Audrey appeared, newly made up, coat over her arm, dark glasses. 'Come on! I'm famished and we need to feed you up.'

'One meal won't make a difference, Mother.'

'It will stretch your stomach and get you growing again.'

Emma smirked her revenge.

Stephen remembered some words. 'I shouldn't be here. I don't belong.'

3

Sixty-eight kilos.

He had dipped into the lower half of his historic range. Within a few weeks, if this continued, he would be the weight he was at Emma's age. Stephen looked at his naked body in the full-length mirror. That stomach was hollowing. That face? – that face was definitely thinner. Those legs and arms looked bony, fragile. It was as if he was growing down instead of up.

'If it worries you, why not see a doctor?' Sarah asked after breakfast, behind the Sunday paper.

'I'm not sure I am worried. Not just yet, anyway. I'll wait. And eat.'

'You did that yesterday.'

'I do it every day. I can't break the habit.'

He made himself more toast, caking it with strawberry conserve. His stomach ached. Something was fretting at his conscience. It came to him over a second cup of coffee. 'I'm afraid I lost my temper with Emma yesterday.'

'You? You never lose your temper with anyone.'

Stephen ignored the hint of contempt. 'Well, this time I did.'

'What happened?'

'I'll get to that. But I think I should phone and apologise.'

Sarah folded her paper and picked up the colour supplement. 'I wouldn't. She's been impossible lately.'

'Civil engineering?'

Sarah looked surprised. 'Is she still going on about that?'

'She told me she's thinking about it. Among other things.'

'Andrew's been getting at her.'

'In order to get at you?'

Sarah flicked through her magazine. 'I'm sure she's chosen it just to spite me.'

'You can't really believe that. She sounded entirely genuine yesterday.'

'I expect you told her it was all right.'

'Well, it's not for me to say, is it? I merely expressed support. She asked how you'd feel about it.'

'What did you say?'

'Naturally, I told her you'd be pleased.'

'Naturally.'

'Anyway, she has a year to change her mind.'

'If Andrew lets her.'

Stephen watched a flock of Canada geese fly over the trees at the end of the road. 'She's thinking of taking a year off.'

Sarah looked up. Stephen crossed his legs. 'Not a year off, exactly. She wants to work for a year. As a barista or something.

Just to see how she feels.'

'How she feels about what?'

'University. The academic life.'

'She must study! She has a brain, if only she'd use it.'

'Even if it's used on civil engineering?'

'I don't want her to fritter away her life making coffees and toasting sandwiches, for God's sake! Or studying something for which she's not suited, just because her father wants revenge.'

'I'm sure Andrew isn't like that.'

'You weren't married to him.'

'It would have looked odd if I was.'

'I know what he's like.'

'Revenge for what?'

'What he thinks we did to him.'

Stephen put a hand to his stomach. 'In my opinion there's no need to make a big thing of this. Plenty of young people take time off. They did it in our day and they do it even more now.'

Sarah looked cross. 'What do you mean, "our day"?' It's still our day, and will be for some time.'

'You know what I mean – since we were students. The world of work has changed completely. There are no more safe jobs; very few good ones either, come to that. Plenty of young people don't decide what they want to do until their early thirties these days.'

'And look what they're doing in the meantime! Earning minimum wage in the kitchens of second-rate restaurants and dependent on handouts from their parents.'

'Is that what's upsetting you? The financial implications?'

'I'm not upset.'

'You sound upset.'

'Take it from me, I'm not!'

They sat, silent, until Stephen cleared his throat. 'I like Emma a lot. She's a clever girl.'

'I do wish she'd learn to talk properly. Everything's at the front of her mouth. They all seem to do it.'

'They?'

'Young people. Especially girls. And that fatuous upward lilt they have these days ... '

'It will pass.' Stephen changed the subject. 'How'd you get on yesterday?'

Sarah glanced at him, crossing her legs, her magazine slipping from her lap. She tut-tutted and picked it up. 'Pretty well. Still a lot to do, of course.'

'Of course.'

'I'd better continue this afternoon. What will you do?'

Stephen shrugged. 'Phone Emma.'

He would have to be patient. It was always the same when one of them was writing a book. They hated talking about what they were doing, resented enquiries about their progress. It was a long solitary struggle with intractable problems and provisional solutions. It made them irritable. It was hard to take. Especially now, at the fag end of the year.

He spoke to Emma that afternoon. She'd clearly forgotten the previous day's incident, but she forgave him anyway. 'Have you had a chance to talk to Mum?'

'Yes, this morning. It went very well. She'll come round to the idea in time.'

'Can I speak to her now?'

'I don't think that would be a good idea, Emma. She's locked herself away.'

Emma sighed into the phone. 'It feels like she's been writing that book forever.'

'She has.'

His lie about Sarah's reaction rekindled his embarrassment about Audrey. And as he put down the phone he remembered his sister. It was about time she made some sort of effort. Her absence at Christmas would be another insult thrown at her mother. Audrey would drink and complain, unable to let it go. Someone – probably he – would have to make the first move.

When Stephen next opened his eyes it was another Monday morning. George came to see him in his office. 'Have you heard?'

'Morning, George. Heard what?'

'More podcasts and video lectures are in the offing. I wonder if we should get a business agent. What do you think?'

'If it means sell-out gigs all over Europe, why not? You must be pleased.'

George ran a fist over his chin. 'I don't know what to think. On the one hand, it means fewer personal appearances in front of the punters, which is fine by me. On the other, we only have to record enough of these shows and we'll be out of a job.'

'You're being uncharacteristically gloomy, George, if I may say so. I like the ways things are going. It makes the best use of everyone's time. We'll be able to give students individual attention. And we'll have more opportunity to work on our own stuff.'

'But if every other university is going the same way ... '

'Then we'd be foolish to miss the boat.'

'It's easy for you to talk. You look good on TV. I look like a strange man who's wandered into the wrong building.'

Stephen wasn't listening. He tugged at the waistband of his trousers, then slipped a finger inside his shirt collar. 'Do I look smaller to you?'

George raised his eyebrows. 'Are you still obsessing about weight?'

'Or bigger?'

'You look exactly the same to me. Of course, in these glasses I can barely see my hand in front of my face.'

'It's like something's gnawing away at me but I don't know what.'

George shuffled about, looked concerned. 'If this really worries you, why not see a doctor?'

Stephen, frowning, came from behind the desk and walked to the window. 'That's what Sarah suggested.'

'There you are, then! Two of the greatest intellects on the face of the planet are agreed. Make them both happy and do what they say.'

'I'll think about it.'

Monday morning wore away.

He'd forgotten about Paul, he remembered. He left a message on his friend's mobile, asking him if he'd like to get together for a drink. 'Call me when you can.'

Stephen took a walk at lunchtime. The day was cold, with bursts of raging wind. The aroma of wet leaves was dark and bitter, and vehicles hissed on wet tarmac. He attacked the city's gradients, walking briskly and at random along residential streets, household bins strewn across the pavements. His legs felt weak and his breath was laboured when he emerged from a side road and found himself in a parade of shops, standing opposite his sister's dry cleaning establishment.

It shocked him. The place was neglected, shabby, resigned to failure. Checking his watch, he wondered if he should give up. It was already one o'clock and he'd have to be getting back. He crossed the road, hesitated near a postbox. A young man carrying garments encased in plastic wrapping emerged from the back room. Stephen pushed through the door, stepping over a pile of tinsel to get to the counter.

'Is Angela here today?'

'Angela?'

'The owner. Angela Ketley.'

'No, mate. I'm on my own today.'

'Do you know when she'll be here?'

'No idea. Sorry. Any message?'

Stephen hesitated. 'No. No message.'

He walked back to the campus and thought how typical it was that his sister should be elsewhere on the one day he decided to pay her a visit. He didn't even have her phone number. Angela had made herself as elusive as it was possible to be in a city she shared with her own brother. 'Horrible, horrible, horrible!'

At a pedestrian crossing he had a bout of dizziness. He leant against a railing while traffic pumped hot fumes into his face. He should have had a bigger lunch. Think big meals – he must remember to think big meals.

Tuesday wore away. Stephen kept an eye out for Jack Caswell, who missed a class, then another. He caught up with him on

Wednesday morning. 'Come to lunch,' he told him.

Jack looked aghast. 'Lunch?'

'If you're free, that is.'

'I don't know ... '

'I'd appreciate it if you could. Come to my office around twelve, will you?' Stephen walked away before his student could object.

Pleased with his own decisiveness, Stephen enjoyed a good morning. During his coffee break he checked his phone. Still nothing from Paul, but Sarah had rung. He called her back.

'I spoke to Lorna,' she told him. 'Paul's away on business. He won't be back until the weekend. She wondered if we wanted to do anything in the meantime.'

'You could see her. I've left a message with him.'

'Oh? What about?'

'I suggested a drink. Just the two of us.'

Silence. Then: 'You're not still worrying about them, are you?'

'Worry is too strong a word. I just thought I could have a quiet conversation, sound him out, that kind of thing.'

Sarah told him it was a bad idea. 'Leave it to me. I'll see Lorna.'

'I thought you didn't have time to see anyone. Your book ... '

After a cough and a pause, Sarah said: 'I must have one night off. And if you're that concerned about them, there's more chance of Lorna saying something than there is of Paul admitting to anything.'

'That's an odd choice of words, isn't it? You make him sound culpable.'

'If there is something wrong it's usually the man's fault. Besides, you know what I mean.'

Afterwards, Stephen searched the internet for the address of Angela's dry cleaning place. When he found her website he was surprised to learn she had three of them. Business had to be good, despite appearances. Three establishments and three phone numbers. He made a note of them all, asking himself why. Phoning her out of the blue – he didn't feel comfortable.

His coffee finished, a sharp pain flashed in his stomach, fading to emptiness. He put it down to hunger. Lunch would be copious, he decided. Big meals, day after day, until he was back to optimum weight.

Jack appeared in his doorway around midday.

'What do you want?' growled Stephen.

Jack took a step back. 'Don't you remember? You asked – '

Stephen smiled. 'Only joking. I'm so glad you could come. Let's get going, shall we?'

They caught the bus to the city centre. A cold wind struck at them from street corners. Stephen rushed Jack to the restaurant he'd chosen. 'I haven't been here for years,' he explained, opening the door. 'My wife and I used to come here often, but then, like the naked nun, we lost the habit. I don't know if the food's still good, but at least it's warm in here.'

Stephen ordered a bottle of an Italian red and poured Jack a glass. 'Read any good books lately?'

'Something on our reading list. *Noah's Arc*, by Noah Tredwell?'

'Interesting choice! And what do you think?'

Jack pursed his lips. 'I really like it, but it's weird, isn't it? All over the place.'

'You should try his new one! I've only just started it, but I can't make sense of it yet. That's one of the reasons I think his work is so good – almost unique. He hasn't caught the fatal disease of so much modern fiction.'

'Overweening underambition?'

Stephen nodded, smiled. 'You have been listening to me, after all. When you turn up, that is.'

Jack turned red, green eyes looking down at his hands. 'I – '

'I supposed you were under the weather. I'm glad you're feeling better.'

Stephen ate as much as he could. The food was as good as he'd remembered. He kept their glasses topped up and they talked about Tredwell and books until it was time for dessert. Throughout, Jack looked tense, occasionally embarrassed. As the wine took hold, his eyes ceased to wander.

'Still thinking of leaving us?' asked Stephen.

Jack, head bowed, toyed with his ice cream. 'I've thought about it a lot and I think I should go.'

Stephen started on his own dessert. 'God! This crêpe is good.' He swallowed a spoonful of cream and autumn berries. 'I'm glad you told me. It's your decision, of course. But I do wish you'd change your mind.'

Jack shrugged, said nothing.

'I don't want to pry but ... is the student counselling service helping you? I was obliged to refer you to them, but I also know they happen to be very good.'

'I don't know ... Maybe ... We've barely got going.'

Stephen nodded. 'These things take time.'

'Yes. Time ...'

Stephen frowned and ate another mouthful of crêpe. 'Look, before we think about you going, suppose you tell me what the problem is. Can you do that?'

Jack pulled a face and became absorbed with his napkin. 'You must know as much as I do. I can't keep up with the others. That's it, really. It feels, like, I'm the odd one out?'

'In what way?'

'In every way! I try to think of something to say, but by the time I've thought of it it's too late. I feel so dumb. Stupid!'

Stephen nodded. 'It's happened to all of us, so I know what you mean. But then, when you think about it, you can't really be stupid, can you? You're here, for a start. You got the grades, you passed the interview, the university invited you because we thought you weren't stupid.'

'The university was wrong.'

'And your schools, too? They got it wrong?'

Jack shrugged his shoulders, his eyes following a young waitress.

'Believe me, Jack, you must be very clever indeed to have got this far by fooling everyone you're intelligent enough to pass their exams. Have you thought of that?'

'But everyone else is so much cleverer than I am.'

'Suppose you let me be the judge of that? Would you believe me if I told you that, so far, you're neither better nor worse than anyone else in your year? It's the truth, I assure you.'

'Then how come everyone knows what to ask and I don't? It feels like they're a year ahead of me.'

Stephen finished his dessert, wiped his mouth. 'Do you know what I think, Jack? I think this is a question of confidence rather than intelligence. You see a couple of confident students who know how to talk and you think they must be geniuses. They're not. Their essays got exactly the same grade as yours.'

'They must have had an off day.'

Stephen picked up an unused fork and tapped it against his knee. Jack sniffed. All at once, Stephen knew who it was he'd heard crying all alone in the toilet.

'Where do you live, Jack?'

'Nottingham.'

'I mean where do you come from? Where's your home?'

'Nottingham. I live at home with my parents.'

'Saves a lot of money.'

Jack nodded.

'Is this the first time you've felt like this?'

'No. I can't remember.'

'I ask because it's not the first time a new student has come to me and told me what you've just said. It can be very hard to adjust to university, especially if you're far from home. You don't have that worry, at least.'

Jack stared at the table.

'Sometimes it takes a whole year before you really begin to feel at ease. My first year was pretty bad. It takes me a long time to make friends. It was only in the third term that I began to enjoy myself.'

Jack looked surprised. 'But you're so talented, you must be! You're a professor, you have ideas, you know what to say, how to think. You write great books.'

'How would you know about my books?'

'I've read a few.'

'You surprise me. Not many people have. You're part of an elite coterie of individuals who managed to get through a book by Stephen Ketley.'

Jack smiled for the first time that Stephen could remember. 'I said I'd read them. I didn't say I'd finished them.'

Stephen laughed. 'You're still way ahead of most people. When's our next class?'

'Monday. I think.'

'I tell you what. Think about what I've said. And think about a question you could ask during class. Or a comment you could make. It doesn't have to be fancy. Just something to get you talking. Practise with a video lecture or two. I'll watch out for you and make time for you to speak without letting the others know. Then, afterwards, we can meet again and see how we feel. How does that sound?'

'I don't know. It's asking a lot of you.'

'And you, don't forget. You've got to think of something interesting to say. I'm counting on it.'

Jack looked doubtful.

'I don't want to force you to do anything you don't want. But do think about it. I'd really hate to lose you. Especially after this interesting discussion. I like your point of view.'

'You do?'

Stephen looked at his watch. ‘Coffee?’

‘Oh! Well ... yes, if you’re having one.’

‘I am. You order. I must just shoot to the lavatory. Besides, I saw you admiring our waitress.’

Stephen climbed the stairs, past doorways marked *Private* and *Staff Only*.

Jack puzzled him. The thought of him weeping like that, locked away in his own little hell, ate at his conscience. Stephen told himself he’d lived long enough to learn that the bowels really are the seat of the emotions. His stomach was jabbing at his complacency. He wondered what it meant. Still, today, for the first time, a little progress had been made. With Jack and with a big meal. At least, it felt like it.

Washing his hands, he stared at his reflection. He felt full, looked thin. His face was the wrong colour – pale, washed out, dark under the eyes. The light wasn’t good – that could be it. And he needed a rest. The end of term loomed with dubious Yuletide promise, shut up with Audrey for days on end, no one to talk to but Ella and Billie. Sarah would be in solitary confinement with her German expressionists. It was hard to know which of them had the worst deal.

Distracted by his sudden gloom, he took a wrong turning and saw Paul Gillespie enter the private dining room. Stephen smiled, a pleasurable warmth surfing over his despondency. Paul was always joking how hard it was to spend his days wining and dining clients. He didn't have problems with weight loss. Paul jogged and gymned his way out of obesity. Tall and slim, he looked good in suits.

Stephen peeked through the glass panel of the door. Paul was wearing his blue pinstripe, the one that made him look like a barrister. 'It's embarrassing enough to be a marketing executive for a tyre manufacturer,' he had told Stephen. 'I damn well refuse to look like one.'

Paul sat down and took a sip of white wine. He stretched out his hand and placed it comfortably on the waiting palm of his companion. They looked at one another and Stephen knew with complete conviction they were in love. He'd once been able to invoke that excited gleam in Sarah's eyes. She had that gleam now. Paul had put it there.

Stephen drew back and leaned against the wall. Suddenly, it was difficult to breathe.

4

'Are you all right, Professor Ketley? You look odd.'

'Yes, yes, I'm fine. Listen, Jack, I've discovered I'm late for an appointment. Would you mind if I left you to your coffee?'

Stephen paid the bill and said goodbye. 'Remember what we discussed.'

It was colder now, the air damp with wintry breath. The crowds, the decorated streets, the buskers – it was all too much, too soon, and he had to steady himself, catch hold of a lamppost, wait for the colours to stop spinning their pain behind his tearful eyes. He rubbed the moisture away on the back of his sleeve, sniffed, chose a street to follow to its bitter end.

The season of good cheer had taken him by surprise. He asked himself what he had to do. 'I have to think about presents ... There's so much to do ... Audrey, Emma. And Sarah ...'

She had admired a silk scarf a while back. Stephen went to the Paul Smith shop and looked for the paisley pattern with a modern twist. It was expensive, so Sarah hadn't bothered. But this was Christmas.

'Would you like it wrapped, Sir?'

'Yes, please. It's a gift.'

He'd put the scarf deep in his bag, so she wouldn't see it when he got home. Stephen buttoned his coat and returned to his office.

His mind felt preternaturally clear. He found a great deal of work to do. There were all those essays to grade. His comments on his students' work were focused, detailed, incisive. He felt pleased, full of energy. He'd stay an extra hour and get through everything that needed to be done.

It certainly felt good to have made a start on those presents.

Desklamp on, he thought about Jack. He hoped the young man would stay. Lunch had revealed curiosity and intelligence beneath all that frightened insecurity. It would be a shame if he lost himself, went to waste. Stephen recalled the sound of tears echoing in the lavatories. Then he found he was crying.

He dried his eyes with a tissue, standing at the window, lights flickering and sweeping through the car park, the roads beyond. Rectangles of night huddled at unlit corners, between buildings. Somewhere behind him a door was slammed, brisk footsteps thudding along the tiles towards the stairs. He recognized Gordon Zellaby's preoccupied tread. Cleaners arrived, trolleys rattling, bin bags swishing.

Time for him to go. He turned off the light and put on his coat in the dark. He said goodnight to the cleaner he knew by sight. At the bus stop he stood at the back of the queue, eyes on the empty football pitch across the street. The floodlights made patterns on the grass. The bus left without him. He stared at the pitch. Then he walked.

He wished he'd thought of gloves. The hand carrying his bag felt frozen. He swapped the bag over to his other side, put his cold hand in his coat pocket. Traffic was crawling on the main road out of town. Drumbeats thumped from open windows, rage rapping in luxury cars. Lights swept over him and travelled on.

'This is a walk thing. This is a walk thing.'

Waiting at kerbs, crossing roads, avoiding unlit bicycles – it was all so simple he didn't have to think. How peaceful to trust to habit and experience. Knowledge on automatic. If only he'd left his bag at the office. He swapped sides, his frozen hand searching for warmth in his pocket.

His legs grew numb. He would have to rest soon or else.

On the Derby road he turned into the entrance way to a block of flats. He looked up at balconied windows dim with light. A car pulled in and dipped down to the car park beneath the building. Stephen followed. There at the corner was the darkness he sought. An unlit space with a flight of cement stairs. Stephen went down.

The tunnel was his shortcut home, its abrupt descent into darkness illuminated midway by a stone-clad vault with a spiralling staircase that led to the street above. Stephen hurried through the dark, pausing at the foot of the staircase to look at the night sky. The remainder of the tunnel was filled with cold silence. Nothing stirred beyond its leaf-fringed mouth.

Stephen mumbled to the rhythm of his tread. 'This is a walk thing ... It feels good to have made a start on the presents ... I need to visit Audrey again before too long ... Sarah will be pleased with the scarf ... I got through those essays much quicker than I thought ... I hope Jack decides to stay ... Giuliana told me I should get my head out of books ... I must weigh myself again tomorrow ... Big meals ...'

He sees Paul walk to the private dining room, his hand take hold of another hand. Stephen's hand around the handle of his bag feels frozen. 'I don't ... want to know! ... I don't ... want to know!' A blaze of colours – aquamarine blue and lemon yellow – explodes in a fevered delirium, fades to awful invading darkness. Its terrible weight spins him to the ground, sends him reeling – reeling and falling.

Cold stone ... dreamless oblivion. Timeless. Nothing.

More nothing.

Then ... hands ...

More hands ...

He can feel hands.

A hand was shaking his shoulder. A hand was on his arm. If only they would leave him alone.

Stephen opened his eyes, pushed himself to a sitting position. A man was crouching over him, his face uncomfortably close to his own. Stephen could see the skin creased around the man's eyes, which were strange, intense, full of wild energy. Broken veins flowered scarlet over his nose, while his lips – thin and bloodless, cracked at the corners – were pulled back, revealing brown oversized teeth and the aroma of warm beer. His hair was the dull yellow of nicotine stain.

The man tilted his head, screwed up his face, his nostrils flaring. 'And you notice the creatures have fled, strangely!'

Stephen recoiled. The voice was half-shriek half-groan. It issued from the man's gaping mouth, but the sound of it surrounded them, echoed and reverberated, forward and back.

'There is vibration in the air – your eyelids hurt! You wonder if the earth is hollow, but then what could happen to the clouds in winter? Do you believe the call of the bird at night spells magic? It is the Sixth Great Extinction! Do you have the words, you ask? Dip your hands in the river of blood if so!'

Stephen had been sprayed with spittle. He tried to stand. The man took hold of his arm, gripping it above the elbow. Stephen was pulled up. The man put his hand on Stephen's chest and pushed. Stephen felt a wall against his back.

The man put his face inches from Stephen's. 'Feel better Friend?' The question was a whisper, sudden and infinitely searching.

Stephen looked around, wondered where he was and how he could get away. 'I must have fainted ... I'm sorry ... I'm all right now.'

'Sureness you feel?'

'Yes, yes, quite sure.'

The man stooped down and handed Stephen his bag. 'Appurtenances of life are vouchsafed to those without knowledge!'

'Thank you. Thank you.'

Stephen rubbed his knee, stumbled away. Beneath a streetlight, he looked back. The man stood watching. He raised a hand. 'There is still time to cross, yet none will do so!' he shouted. Behind him, the tunnel gaped.

Stephen limped around the corner.

The streets that led home appeared unchanged since the morning. The same old houses awash in dead leaves and Christmas decorations, the same old lives. He opened his front door.

'What happened to you?'

Sarah's question asked more than he was able to answer. 'Oh, nothing much. I fell down carrying this bag. Then I met a strange man.'

'Your coat's filthy.'

Stephen looked at his mud-spattered coat. It made him feel obscurely guilty. He asked, bright with shame: 'Have you eaten?'

'Yes. I was working when I heard you come in. I'll get back to it if you're all right.'

'Yes, do. Don't mind me.'

Sarah turned, hesitated. 'Are you sure you're all right?' Her eyes narrowed. 'You look odd.'

'Odd?'

'Are you still losing weight?'

'You're looking at the new Grant Williams.'

Stephen went early to bed, felt his stomach rise and fall with each cycle of breath. He feigned sleep as soon as he heard Sarah climb the stairs. He listened to her familiar movements, the sliding of the wardrobe doors, cleaning her teeth in the open bathroom. She came to bed, turned her back, knees pulled up, hoarding her body beneath the quilt.

He opened his eyes and thought about love.

'We lie here together like adjoining secrets. How did it come to this? Of what bad thing is this the logical conclusion?'

He had known them both, Andrew and Sarah. Not well, not as friends like ... not as friends ...

Single, Stephen is ambitious. He takes care to see and be seen. Socializing and networking are as important as professional skills and scholarly output in the academic life. He plays the game as well as anyone. It's a game he finds he enjoys. Soon, he has made a name for himself, become popular. Talking effortlessly, a drink in one hand and an eye on the future, he's secure enough to feel sorry for those on the edge of the crowd, who stand mute with fear in the face of so much social mystery.

He has, from time to time, found himself looking at Sarah across a crowded room. 'Andrew and I are having a Christmas party,' she tells him. 'Do come.'

'I'm afraid I can't. Previous engagement.'

'Another time, perhaps.'

'Yes, please.' They both smile.

Andrew turns out to be a civil engineer. 'Just setting up on my own. Freelance.'

'Sounds exciting.'

'Nervewracking more like. Still, it's what I want.'

'Good luck.'

Emma is a young child in another room, to whom Stephen gives little thought. 'She's asleep,' Sarah tells him, one evening, when he finds himself the only invitee.

'Finally!' adds Andrew. 'Would you like another drink?'

While Andrew heads for the kitchen, Stephen turns to Sarah. 'I'm glad things are going well with the new business. It must be a relief. You should both be feeling very proud.'

Sarah, silent, walks over and takes him in her arms. Her kiss

– warm and passionate – lacks all inhibition. She presses herself against him. He can't help responding. When she releases him, she looks him in the eyes for a moment's eternity, walks away. Andrew reappears. 'Here we are.'

'Yes,' says Stephen. 'Here we are.'

They do not meet for weeks. Sarah is away at a conference. He's preoccupied with his parents. Weekends at Matlock watching Audrey descend into self-pity and whiskey, his father powerless to help, shutting himself away with the piano and songs that won't come.

Then, one evening, Sarah appears on his doorstep. 'Where's the bedroom?'

Stephen sighed. 'I'm lying in it, with you.' His wife had fallen asleep, he could tell. He knew her breathing. She'd turned over so her knees pressed against his thigh.

The familiar pressure of her body was casual, neither intended nor unintended. Unlike before. He thought of all the times they had met in strange rooms and out of the way places. How many had there been? He had felt bad about it. Felt bad for Andrew, whom he liked. He'd found out later – been told – that the marriage was in trouble, that Andrew wanted a divorce, but it didn't seem to help. The situation needed fixing. All that ambiguity wasn't good for anyone. There was Emma to think about ...

Sex with Sarah is furious, elemental, a raging battle that leaves them exhausted. Their desire for one another is flattering, frightening. Intimacy has to be grasped at each occasion, for their times alone are rare and precious. They aren't like other couples, can't do normal things out in the open, have to hide themselves away. Only when the divorce is on can they show themselves to the world.

They marry as soon as Sarah is divorced. Stephen does not invite his parents – too much pain at home, too much alcohol at the wedding. Angela is otherwise engaged.

He invites Giuliana. An email sent to her old address follows her tumultuous life, finds her miraculously, in Rome. He is astonished to see her as beautiful as he remembered. He takes her aside, his arm through hers.

'Why did you invite me?' she asks.

'Why did you say yes?'

Neither of them answers.

'What are you doing now?'

'I live in Rome, these past years. I have a newspaper column. I write film scripts with my partner.'

'Sounds wonderful. Are you happy?'

Giuliana shrugs. 'Some things yes, other things no. Happiness is too small a word for real life. And you? What are you doing now?'

'Marrying, as you see.'

'Yes. Why?'

Stephen laughs. 'Because I want to. Because I want to be with Sarah.'

Giuliana looks at Sarah across the room, says nothing.

Stephen drew back the quilt and held his breath.

'I hope you'll both be very happy,' Giuliana tells him at the door, waiting for her taxi.

'You don't sound convinced we shall be.'

'I am not convinced because you are not convinced.'

'How can you tell?'

'You once thought we were in love.'

'A long long time ago.'

'Not so long. I don't think you've changed.'

'Don't you? I thought I had.'

'I wonder if you ever will. I hope so.'

'You don't sound convinced of that, either. I remember ... I remember you once told me I should get my head out of books.'

She smiles, shakes her head. 'Out of other people's books.' A car pulls up. 'Is that my taxi? So soon?'

But it isn't her taxi. It is Andrew, with Emma in his arms.

Stephen stands at the front door, tells himself to act natural. 'Andrew! And how are you, little Emma?' But Emma will have none of it, hiding her face in her father's arms.

'Is Sarah around?' Andrew looks at Giuliana, then stares into the house, at the people talking, at their plates of food and their glasses of wine. He looks – how? – sad and humiliated beneath his bluster of hurt pride. His face is flushed with drink, his eyes bloodshot.

'Andrew, perhaps you didn't understand, but this is our – our wedding day.'

'Oh, I know that, don't you worry. I just wanted to bring the car over and show Emma her mother.'

'The car?' Stephen looks at the old Volkswagen parked crazily, one wheel at an angle on the pavement.

'Yes, it is Sarah's after all, as she keeps reminding me. I've had the brakes seen to. That's on me, by the way. Think of it as a wedding present.'

Stephen glances over his shoulder at Giuliana, embarrassed by her presence, her dawning comprehension of who this is.

'Stephen, darling! What are you doing all this time at the front door?' It is Sarah, come to seek him out and detach him from Giuliana, drink in hand, smiling that smile, her face ready to be kissed. She sees his confusion, then Andrew. Her face hardens. 'Andrew! I consider your presence here to be in very bad taste.'

Andrew laughs. 'I don't think you're in any position to pronounce on matters of taste, Sarah. Aren't you going to invite us in? This is Emma, your daughter – remember? Emma, this is

Mummy. She's married a new husband today. Uncle Stephen. You remember him, don't you? That nice man we welcomed in our home.

'Andrew – '

'So, Sarah, how does it feel to be a decent, respectable married woman? You must find the change quite bracing.'

Sarah looks over her shoulder at the guests, stands at Stephen's shoulder, barricading the door, screening impropriety. 'What do you want, Andrew?'

'Want? Why, nothing! You know me. I'm the discarded husband who keeps on giving. Here are the car keys.' He offers them up.

Sarah hesitating, Stephen takes them. 'Thank you. Would you like ... ?'

'No, he would not like! Thank you for the car, Andrew. Now, please leave. You've made your point.'

'Have I? What point is that, exactly?'

'That our happiness has ... coincided with your disappointment. You seem to forget it was the other way around for many years.'

Andrew deliberately misunderstands. 'Many years? You mean – you mean you and he were committing adultery in motel bedrooms and parked cars for *years*? Just think, I had no idea! The faithful little wife, I thought, working hard, committed to husband and daughter, and all the time she's dreaming of her next tryst with another lover ...'

Stephen takes a step forward. 'Andrew, this isn't helping ...'

'Speak for yourself! It's helping me enormously. And Emma. She wants to know what kind of a mother she has really. It's quite an education, isn't it, Darling?'

Stephen looks back over Sarah's head, sees they have an audience. Giuliana closes the hall door on the crowd of ogling guests.

Sarah smiles a tight little smile. 'Well, you've certainly achieved what you set out to accomplish, Andrew. Now, would you kindly leave?'

Andrew, suddenly, embarrassingly, is tearful, his face childlike in its anguish, his voice rising an octave. 'What you've done! ... What you've done to us ... Your own daughter!' He sways, puts his hand to Emma's face, already obscured by her hair, long and dark, shielding her from the iniquity of her own mother.

'Andrew ...'

Strangely triumphant through his tears, Andrew steps back, takes a good look at Stephen. 'If it can happen to me, it can happen to you! Think about that!'

'Will you kindly go! Now! This minute!'

Stephen, shocked by her vehemence, looks at Sarah, at

Andrew. At Giuliana, standing against the door to the sitting room. Sarah brushes her aside, returns to her guests. 'Sorry about that, everyone!' He sees her back disappear as the door swings shut.

Stephen lay still as Sarah turned over, her face close to his, her breath warm on his face.

Later, when they are all pretending to have forgotten, Giuliana pulls him aside, asks him questions. 'Why is her husband so sad, so hurt? What happened?'

'He's not her husband, I am! He wanted a divorce long before I came on the scene. Now he's feeling sorry for himself. Perhaps the truth is too much for him.'

'What truth?'

'That he's finally got what he wants.'

'And so has his wife.'

'*My* wife.'

'Are you sure everything's all right? I mean, there's nothing you could have done ...?'

'Quite sure. I acted as best as I could.'

They watch Sarah laughing with her guests. 'Do you really love her?'

'What kind of question is that? Of course I do!'

Giuliana arches an eyebrow. 'I hardly know her, but already I don't see how you could. For her, love is provisional, like she'd change a dress that no longer pleases her.'

'Giuliana –'

'You saw what she was like with her husb– Andrew and her daughter. She didn't say a word to her little girl. Not even a smile. It makes me shiver!'

'We arranged between us all that Emma would be with her father. It seemed the best thing.'

'The best thing for whom?'

'For everyone. Giuliana, why are you questioning me like this? You don't know any of these people. I do. You can't just appear in our midst, knowing nothing, and pronounce on our lives – on my life. You know nothing of my life.'

'I'm here because you invited me, remember? And I know you.'

'You used to. Not anymore. People change. I've changed and you've changed. And what about your own life? Are you so perfect?'

Giuliana laughs, sips her drink. 'No, I'm not perfect. In some ways my life is a mess. I try to remain faithful ...'

'Faithful to what?'

'An idea. To myself. To love.'

'Love!'

Giuliana looks puzzled, sad. 'This is your wedding day, Stephen. Don't you believe in love?'

Stephen put a hand to his stomach. Sarah mumbled something in her sleep. He turned his head and felt her hair against his face.

Andrew's distress could not simply be dismissed, forgotten. Ignoring it meant ignoring himself.

The bright guilty signs of his own betrayal waft upon his memory. Sarah's interminable book. All her sudden absences, those plausible justifications and explanations. Her abrupt change of clothes, her need for another shower. The remade bed. He grips the side of the mattress. This bed, too?

'I don't feel comfortable about this.'

'Please don't feel concerned,' Sarah tells him, undressing.

'It doesn't seem right.'

'It's my bed. Andrew and I don't sleep together. We haven't for a long time.'

'Even so.'

'Don't be such a prude, Stephen! I've told you it's all right. Look at me!'

Sarah, in new lingerie, lies on the bed. She lifts a stockinged leg, ready for battle. Her body, her secret smile, an unanswerable argument. All-conquering Eros. Stephen is slain. 'Thy thighs are white horses yoked to a chariot of kings.'

This bed, too? All those departures of his – to work, to his mother – how eagerly they must have waited for him to be gone.

Whispered conversations in his own home, his own bed. Their confidential arrangements sped on their way by his unsuspecting trust. He had been stupid.

'If it can happen to me, it can happen to you! Think about that!'

Stephen thought about it. 'Another lover,' Andrew had said. An obvious lie, or an exaggeration at any rate. There had been no others. And what if there had? The marriage was over in all but name, all but Emma. So Sarah had told him.

After the wedding, he phones Giuliana. 'Can we meet before you leave the country?' He hears her breathing at the other end of the line. 'Giuliana?'

'Come to my hotel.'

London is dirty and wet. Giuliana does not like it. 'I want to go home. There is no rain like Roman rain.'

'I always remember Florence when I think of you.'

'Do you often think of me?'

'Infrequently. Regularly.'

'My parents still own the villa. They may sell.'

'Don't let them! Tell them it would make a young Englishman they do not know very sad.'

Giuliana smiles. 'I hope they keep it, too.'

They go to lunch. 'I hope you didn't mind my calling you.'

'I was surprised. I thought you were on your honeymoon!'

'That's for later. When term ends.'

'Will you go away?'

'Yes. Somewhere warm, with no people.'

'Florence?'

'No, not Florence. Giuliana, I'm ... sorry about what happened. With Andrew, I mean. I'm sorry I lost my temper.'

'Did you lose your temper?'

'I thought I did. I'm glad you didn't notice.'

She laughs, pulls a face at the soup. 'This is supposed to be minestrone?'

The meal goes by too quickly. Stephen is anxious, pained by a strange yearning. 'I know you so well, yet I hardly know you at all. I feel I want to ask you a thousand questions, but I don't know where to begin. I want you to tell me all about yourself, everything you have done every day since Florence. I want to know about your work and where you live – all the rooms and the garden and the colours of your days.'

She tells him about her flat, her work, about everything except Tonio, her partner. Stephen remains unsure what that appellation actually implies, and why she is guarded. About her work she is more forthcoming. 'I love writing the scripts. We've not done many but they have been filmed. Perhaps you have seen them?'

'I doubt it, I'm afraid. I don't go to the cinema – there's never the time.'

'The journalism is less enjoyable, but it makes me feel I am contributing something in difficult times. It's very hard to be serious about anything today. People won't let you. Do you write?'

'Oh, yes. A few books on the postmodern novel. One on Edith Wharton.'

'Your thesis?'

'Yes.'

'I remember! And your other writing?'

'You always told me I needed to get my head out of books.'

'I always told you to get your head out of other people's books – not your own.'

Stephen crosses his legs, picks up the napkin that has slipped to the floor at his feet. 'It's not been possible, I'm ashamed to say.'

'You always wanted to write.'

'Did I? I don't remember.'

'It's a pity.'

'My career ...'

'Oh yes, your career, and now your marriage. There are always things to prevent us from doing what we should be doing, what would make us fulfilled.'

'I'm not unhappy.'

'I said fulfilled.'

'I aim to be, now. And are you fulfilled?'

Giuliana shrugs, considers. 'Not really – as much as I can be. So many of one's choices are dictated by circumstances, other people. It's important to exercise control over what can be controlled. Autonomy. My life is chaotic, but there's not much I can do about it now.'

'I'm sad you're leaving tomorrow. Flying out of my life forever.'

'Perhaps not forever. But I do need to leave. Don't you agree?'

They look at one another. 'Yes.'

Stephen turned his face to a long and sleepless night. The dark corners of the bedroom grew pale with the dawn.

He decided he was far from all right.

5

Stephen sat on a wooden chair wedged between a photocopier and the open door. The window to his left looked out over rooftops and chimney stacks. The sky was overcast, sullen with winter. He wished the window were open, despite the cold; the air was thick with the smell of chemicals.

He'd been directed to a pokey little office at the back of the building on the first floor. He sat uncomfortably in his overcoat and wondered what he was doing here. The room was a mess. The desk in the opposite corner was covered in papers, a tiny artificial Christmas tree, an old desk-tidy crammed with pens, overflowing with paperclips. Backed on to the desk, there was a stained table with a battered kettle and a box of teabags, beneath which the leads to the kettle, the phone, and an angle lamp hung in knots on their way to a multigang nailed to the wall. The lino floor was littered with old Post-its and sugar-cube wrappers. The peeling mint-green walls were plastered with spreadsheets, postcards, and a photo-calendar featuring someone he should no doubt have recognized.

From the stairwell outside the door he could hear voices and the hum of machinery. Somewhere a door banged shut. He heard footsteps on the stairs and his sister came in.

She didn't see him there, tucked behind the door. When she went to the desk he heard her sigh. She deposited her bag on the swing chair jammed against the back wall. Then she turned towards the kettle and caught sight of him. She took a step back, staring, her hand to her breast.

She looked older after however many years it had been. Her brown eyes gazed at him in tired wonder, and her hair blown by the wind was tangled, unkempt. Her face, he realized, was the face of someone with troubles they'd learned to live with.

'I'd forgotten what you looked like! What are you doing here?'

Her voice was familiar, strange. He looked at her and didn't know what to say. He shrugged, continued to look at her.

Defensive, suspicious – he couldn't make up his mind – Angela removed her raincoat and held it over her arm while she leaned against the desk. The cold air that had clung to her from the streets crept over him. A minute later he watched as she closed the door and made them both a mug of tea. They sipped together in silence, Angela staring out the window, Stephen looking at the calendar. 'Who's that?' he asked, nodding at the photograph.

Angela looked blank. 'Is that what you came here to find out?'

'He seems familiar.'

'It's Buzz. He had it made up. It's easy to do these days.'

Stephen gazed at Buzz rampant, acoustic guitar held high, leather hat pulled low. 'I didn't recognize him. He looks so young.'

'He used an old photo.'

Stephen nodded. That sounded like Buzz. 'How is he?'

Angela sipped her tea. 'Do you really want to know?'

Stephen didn't answer.

There was a movement outside the window. A carrion crow settled on a cluster of chimneys, scrabbling at its toehold, wings raised in portentous arcs. Stephen pointed, eyes bright with manufactured enthusiasm. '"Once upon a midnight dreary, while I pondered weak and weary ..." Do you remember?'

'Poe? The Raven?'

Stephen nodded. He held his mug against his cheek, felt the warmth suffuse his face. 'Sorrow for the lost Lenore ...'

'I never did like Poe.'

'It gave you the creeps when Dad recited it at bedtime.'

'Bedtime was always creepy in that house.'

'Was it?' Stephen leaned forward, put his empty mug on the table. 'How's business?'

'Fine.' Angela glanced about the room. 'You mustn't judge by this. Blame the previous owner. We'll be redecorating.'

'Three places now, I gather.'

'Tomorrow, the world.'

Stephen stood up, sat down, looked at his sister.

'And how are you?' asked Angela, staring into her tea.

'Oh, yes, you know, fine.'

'How's Sarah?'

'Busy. Enjoying herself.'

Angela looked at him.

'Work's going well,' he told her, filling the anxious silence.

'You and your books!'

The chemical smell intensified. Stephen looked at the window, saw the crow flap out of sight. 'I suppose you're used to the lack of oxygen.'

'The window doesn't open.'

Stephen's stomach rumbled. He felt hot in his coat. 'I just came over on an impulse. I'm glad you were in.'

'It's been a long time.'

'I have tried before.'

'Oh?'

'The other week. You weren't here.'

'I didn't know.'

'I ... er ... I just thought I'd come over, you know, on the off chance.'

Angela put down her mug, turning her chair to face him. 'Is there something the matter?'

'Oh, no, nothing's the matter. Does there have to be

something the matter for me to come and see you?'

'Then what do you want?'

'Want?'

His sister's face looked hard suddenly, closed to feeling. 'We never did see much of one another, Stephen. Whenever you did put in an appearance it was generally because you wanted something – or wanted me to do something.'

Stephen wondered if that were true. 'I don't recall.' He leaned forward, held his face in his hands, felt the warmth of his enclosed breath pass through his fingers. He spoke quietly. 'How did we get like this, Angela? We used to be close. I thought we were. What happened?'

Angela crossed her legs, hands tucked under her thighs. 'Nothing happened.'

Stephen looked up, his eyes straying to that stupid calendar with its fatuous face. 'Then what?'

Angela appeared to think, hesitate. 'It's been you, Stephen.'

'Me?'

'Didn't you know?'

'Didn't I know what?'

'You didn't want me around anymore.'

Stephen sat up, his body taut. 'That's not true! I wanted to see you. Goodness knows –'

Angela shook her head. 'It's true, believe me! A person knows when they're not wanted. So I gave up on you.' She got to her feet, leant against the desk, folding her arms. 'My God! The things I did to get your approval! Everything was always my fault. Audrey was always "Stephen this" and "Stephen that." But you! You did nothing! One day it dawned on me how stupid I'd been. I'd believed everything you all told me about myself, swallowed the words you put in my mouth, the lies ...'

Stephen felt something hot mount within his chest. He slipped a finger behind the waistband of his trousers, felt the ease with which he could move it around. His stomach seemed to dip away beneath him.

'Are you all right?' Angela had watched him. Her frown expressed anger, not sisterly concern. 'You look odd.'

Stephen smiled. 'So people keep telling me.'

'They're right.'

Stephen looked away, his eyes ranging over the littered lino. 'What about Audrey?'

Angela stiffened. 'What about her?'

'What happened between you two?'

'Nothing happened. You know what she thinks of me. She's always blamed me for her depression, her career gone to pot. While you could do no wrong. You just floated above it all.'

Stephen raised a hand to his face, palm against his cheek. 'Floated above it all?'

'Like you float above everything. I wonder if you feel anything half the time. It's like you don't know how.'

'You're so wrong! It's like ...' He couldn't think what it was like.

'I don't know why you're so surprised. None of you thought I'd ever amount to anything. How do you think that felt?'

'That was only because you were so erratic. You went from one thing to another, didn't settle, didn't apply yourself ...' Stephen stopped, took a deep breath. He looked at his sister and shrugged. 'I'm sorry.'

'Yeah, well ... You'd have been erratic if you were me. It was easy for you – always was. You never stopped to consider what I wanted, what I was going through. I stopped hoping a long time ago that any of you would realize that not everything that's gone wrong is entirely my fault.'

Stephen remembered Audrey's dismissal of his sister the last time he saw her, with Emma. 'I realize it, Angela, believe me, I do. Only the other day with Mother ...'

Angela looked irritated, curious. 'She's still at it, then?'

Stephen pulled a face. 'Audrey's Audrey, of course. There's nothing either of us can do about that.'

'No. How is the old cow?'

'Same as ever. A little more so every day.'

'I always said she'd turn into Norma Desmond.'

'She's not quite that bad.'

'Not yet. I haven't seen her since God knows when.'

'I know. Would you like to? With me? We could go up on the train.'

Angela looked doubtful. 'She still drinking?'

Stephen shrugged. 'It's under control. More or less.'

'I don't think I'm ready for Audrey under control.'

'It's Christmas. Please think about it.' He knew immediately that he had found exactly the wrong words to say.

'I *have* thought about it, Stephen! I've thought about it for years!'

Angela moved, pushed her empty mug across the table, clinking it against the kettle. 'God! You people! You'll never change! It's always me that has to do something, never you or Audrey. All you need do is forgive – Audrey with that pained magnanimity of hers, which never lasts.' She picked up her coat, snatched at her bag on the chair. 'I'm going to eat. If you want to come with me, fine. If you don't, that's fine too. I don't care one way or the other.'

'Angela!'

Her shoes thumped on the echoing staircase, backed by the sounds of dry cleaning. Stephen sighed, followed, stood on the pavement, looking about. Angela was nowhere in sight.

He had not handled things well.

He went back to work. The afternoon turned to darkness and cold. His bus home was crammed with students and late-night shoppers. The woman next to him coughed in his ear.

He phoned Audrey that evening. He heard the clink of a glass and the sound of a hasty swallow.

'Stephen! How wonderful of you to phone.'

Stephen marvelled how Audrey always managed to imply she was neglected by everyone. 'I saw Angela today.'

'Angela?'

'Your daughter.'

'Oh, *that* Angela! What did she have to say for herself?'

'Nothing much. She's fine. Business is going well. I just thought you'd like to know.'

'Thank you, dear.'

'She asked after you.'

'I'm surprised she still remembered who I was.'

'Don't be like that, Mother. I want us to try to get along.'

'Meaning I don't? I'm sure I've not done anything ...'

Stephen held the phone away from his ear while Audrey went into one of her rambles. He knew them all by heart. Always the victim, the innocent ready to forgive and forget, refusing responsibility for everything except her success.

'That's fine, Mother,' he told her, out of patience. 'Listen to me ... listen!'

'Don't shout! I'm not deaf.'

Her voice grew faint. He could picture her sitting next to the phone in the hall, lifting a glass of something, frowning when she found it empty save for the ice cubes. 'I'm sorry, Mother, I didn't mean to shout. But I need you to listen. I have an idea. I thought ... I thought how nice it would be if we had some family thing at Christmas. All of us. Angela as well, if I can persuade – if she's free. What do you think?'

Audrey became excited. 'I do love a traditional Christmas! We could sing carols and go to midnight mass. Have a proper Christmas dinner, with presents under the tree. Just like we used to!'

Stephen couldn't recall anything quite like that. Audrey was always elsewhere in the holidays, entertaining others, until she couldn't manage it anymore, and then ... 'Good! I'll talk to Angela.'

'What about Bing? And Sarah?'

'I don't know about Bing – Buzz, I should say. I don't know how things stand with him and Angela. As for Sarah ...'

'Yes?'

His secret scuttled to the front of his mind. For one crazy moment he was tempted to tell Audrey everything. That Sarah had betrayed him as she had betrayed Andrew, that all was up between them, that things would turn nasty, as they always do.

'Sarah's very busy with her book. She needs to spend the holiday finishing it off. But I'm sure she'll come for the day, at least.'

'Do tell her to try, Stephen! It's not much to ask. I like a house full of people at Christmas. I wonder if Emma would be interested?'

'I'll ask her, too. I don't know who she'll be staying with.'

'Poor sweet girl! Imagine growing up in a broken home, Stephen ...'

'I don't have to imagine.'

'What was that ...?'

'Nothing. Leave things to me. I'll see what can be done. Now, how are things with you and what have you been up to?'

'Oh, nothing much ever happens here ...'

Stephen listened as Audrey talked herself out. He remembered the furious arguments between his parents, the slammed doors, the night he found his mother drunk and unconscious on the kitchen floor. Angela had screamed in the night with bad dreams for what felt like most of his childhood ... No, nothing much ever happened there.

Afterwards, he stood at the door to the study. He heard Sarah typing. He made some tea and brought it to her. 'I saw my sister today.'

'Was she pleased to see you?'

'Difficult to say. She was rather defensive. She gave me the impression that things between the two of them are coming to a crisis.'

'From what you say, Buzz is not the kind of man who deals with a crisis when he can avoid it.'

'Sometimes avoiding a thing is the best option. Until you know what it is you want.'

Sarah shrugged, looked at her computer screen.

'I also spoke to Audrey. About Christmas, mostly. We might try to have a family do. Including Angela, if I can persuade her.'

'Really?' Sarah was reading what she'd written.

'I'd like it if you came too.'

'I can hardly wait.'

'Of course, with all that Christmas cheer and family at full throttle, it would be better if we stayed over for a few days.'

'I've already told you –'

'I know, but in the circumstances I thought you could at least find it in your heart to do this one thing for me.'

Sarah looked at him.

Stephen got up to go. 'Did you arrange anything with Lorna?'

'Lorna? Oh, no, not yet. It was more difficult than we thought.'

'Did she say anything?'

'I didn't ask over the phone.'

'Paul never phoned me back.'

'Didn't he?'

'It's odd. He always has before.'

'Perhaps Lorna said something to him.'

'How could she if you haven't already mentioned the subject?'

'Yes. You're right, of course. Oh well! He's away on business, apparently.'

'Apparently?'

'That's what she told me. Don't you remember?'

That night, he lay in bed and waited for Sarah to go to sleep. It took, he thought, a little longer than usual. Once he could hear her steady breathing, he went quietly to the study and turned on her computer. The white light from the screen shone through the room. He sat down, waited for a car to pass on the road outside. When he opened the files for her book, he took a deep breath. It seemed to him it was more or less finished. Sarah had been working on the final pages that evening. Of course, there's always revision and correction. But it was all there, including the final chapter. She never worked on the final chapter until she was happy with everything else. Things were much more advanced than he had been led to believe.

He checked her emails, found nothing. She wasn't that stupid. She had always been careful, he remembered.

George was waiting for him in his office the next morning. 'Have you heard?'

'Morning, George. Heard what?'

'Zellaby's resigned.'

Stephen dropped his bag on the desk. 'Resigned!'

George looked gratified. 'There's an email about it. Personal reasons, it says.'

'Gordon's resigned? I can't believe it! Where's he going?'

George shrugged. 'I don't think he's going anywhere. His health, you know.'

Stephen joined George at the window, his eyes on the car park. 'I had no idea! He never said anything to me. Did he to you?'

'No. I don't think anyone knew. Not even him.'

'Does he say what's wrong?'

George shook his head. 'You know Zellaby. Plays things close to his chest. Obviously something serious.' He looked at Stephen. 'This is a wonderful chance for you, Stephen.'

Stephen nodded, then took in what he'd heard. 'What do you mean?'

'For promotion, of course. Don't tell me it hadn't crossed your mind.'

'What about you? You're just as likely ...'

George laughed, shook his head. 'I don't fit, old boy. I'm more of your maverick genius than a pro vice-chancellor. Whereas you – you've got the icy mind required to keep the administrators at bay.'

Stephen pursed his lips. 'God, this is really a shock. I don't know what to say. Is he in?'

'I don't know. I presume so. Why?'

'I'd like to talk to him.'

'Go careful. This is a political thing now. Anything could happen.' George narrowed his eyes, looked Stephen up and down. 'Are you all right? You look – well – odd.'

'Odd?'

'You've been looking odd these past several days. Is anything the matter? How's your weight?'

'Stabilized,' Stephen lied. 'Neither up nor down.'

'Good. Is anything else bothering you?'

Stephen glanced at George. 'Nothing I can talk about. Thanks for asking.'

George opened his mouth, said nothing, turned to leave. 'You know where I am. Propping up the bar at the Kean's Head.'

Stephen dropped by Zellaby's office that afternoon. 'Got a minute, Gordon?'

Zellaby was riffling through a desk drawer. 'I've ten of them, and welcome. I had some fruit pastilles in here at one time, but ... I give up.'

Stephen sat down. 'I got your news. I'm terribly sorry. What's wrong?'

Zellaby smiled. 'I imagine that's the question on everybody's lips. Everybody's *concerned* lips.'

'Of course, if you don't want to say ...'

Zellaby waved a dismissive hand. 'I was diagnosed with a brain disease that means fundamentally I must change my life – whatever little there remains of it. Don't ask me what it's called. It's polysyllabic, multihyphenated and all in German. I defy anyone to remember it, even if they haven't got it.'

Stephen frowned. 'And is there no hope?'

'None whatsoever, he replied bravely. My mind is going, Stephen. Specifically, my memory. It fades in and out.' He narrowed his eyes. 'Have you noticed anything?'

Stephen lied. 'No, I haven't.'

Zellaby nodded, looked at him, smiled suddenly. 'So, you see, I must flee these hallowed precincts before I become a slobbering embarrassment. If only other academics I could mention would do the same.'

'Gordon, I don't know what to say. Really.'

'Nothing much to say, surely?'

Stephen shook his head. 'How's Anthea taking it?'

'Like the trooper she is. She's already investigating stair lifts and straitjackets, bless her.'

In the ensuing silence Stephen wondered at the human capacity to cope with devastation and then buckle under trifles.

Gordon outside a university would be a fish out of water. Not only was he a first-class scholar, he was also an accomplished and respected administrator – a rare combination. And now that wonderful brain of his had let slip its treacherous betrayal, poisoning all that was good and sublime and recognizably Professor Gordon Zellaby.

Gordon was staring at his hands. 'It's ironic, when you come to think of it. As I've grown older I've found more and more things it's important not to remember. My whole past sometimes feels like a deadly trap. If only we could know at the time that everything we do comes back to haunt us – torment us, even. Then we wouldn't be half so bad as we are, don't you think?'

'I can't imagine you've ever done anything you should be ashamed of.'

Gordon laughed. 'That makes me out to be rather dull. But I'm not talking about high-end immorality. I can assure you I haven't murdered, raped or pillaged. Not literally, anyway. It's the little things that bother me. An unkind word. Or a particular humiliation as a child that shouldn't matter to me now, but rankles in my memory ...' Gordon smiled a wry Zellaby smile. 'But not for much longer, the medics tell me. I shall be free of all regrets and all guilt. You must almost envy me, Stephen. I shall float above my life with sublime insouciance.'

'You're very persuasive, I must say.'

Gordon looked around the office, sighed. 'I shall miss this place. Miss the work.'

'You'll have to become an independent scholar, Gordon. Work at home and revolutionize Shakespearean studies.'

'Now *you're* forgetting: I already have! And I don't know how much time there is left, *compos mentis*-wise.'

'Is there no definite prognosis?'

Gordon shook his head. 'It's incredibly uncertain. Sometimes decline is sudden and steep, other times there's a kind of ... what do they call it? ...' He snapped his fingers, closed his eyes, frowning. 'When someone has cancer that gets better on its own ...'

'Remission?'

'That's it! Remission. Sounds like prison, doesn't it? Which is why I shall be dandling grandchildren on my knee.'

'I hope and trust we'll be seeing a lot more of you while – while we can?'

'By all means. I'm not dead yet. How's Sarah?'

'Oh! She's fine, as far as I'm aware.'

'Don't you know?'

'She's working on her book.'

'Ah! A life behind closed doors. Tell her to get out and enjoy herself once in a while.'

'Yes. I will.'

'You should too. Is everything all right? You've been looking a little odd lately.'

'Odd?'

'Like a boxer dead on his feet.'

'I don't know. There's a lot going on at the moment.'

'To which I've just added.' Zellaby looked at his watch. 'Ten minutes are up. I must to my next engagement. We'll get together soon, Stephen. And if I forget, don't hesitate to remind me. Or Anthea, if need be. I shan't take offence.'

'I'll look forward to it, Gordon.'

Zellaby called him back at the door. 'I shall certainly put in a good word for you, Stephen.'

'A good word?'

'About the job. If you're interested. I can't guarantee anything, of course, but my opinion still counts for something.'

'Do you think I'm up to it, Gordon?'

Zellaby looked at him shrewdly. 'Don't you?'

6

Stephen glanced at the clock where it hung above Jack, who sat slumped over his iPad, alone in the highest tier of the lecture theatre, head in hand.

The end of the class was nigh.

Stephen shuffled his sheaf of notes, picked up his satchel beneath the chair. His belt buckle slid about his midriff. His stomach felt tense with emptiness. Still two hours before lunch.

He cleared his throat, dry from forty minutes' worth of recycled improvisation. 'So that's about it for today, unless someone has anything they want to say.'

He watched as they fidgeted and typed and whispered. They'd been miserably uninspired this morning. He hoped it wasn't his fault. *Hamlet* might be to blame, but he preferred to think it was a weekend of intense study and overindulgence that had sapped their intellectual energies.

'Nothing?'

He looked at their faces – expressionless, tired, preoccupied – and tried not to feel despondent.

'Okay, then, let me ask you something. Most of you will have seen the play in one version or another. How long does *Hamlet* last on the stage?'

Jenny, eager as always, smiled and raised a hand. 'Four hours?'

'Yes, about that. So we sit around for four hours watching Hamlet, Prince of Denmark prevaricate, change his mind, put on a play and generally arse around and not do anything much until the final ten minutes. Why doesn't he just get on with it? What's his problem?'

Stephen stood up, stretched, put his hands in his pockets, his eyes on his shoes as he paced circles around his chair. Silence. He looked up. 'Don't all speak at once! Come on, someone must have an idea! Yes, Liz?'

'He's in a chronic state of indecision? Like, psychologically, he can't get his head around what needs to be done?'

'And why's that?'

'Like ... it's a sexual thing with his mother? If it was anyone but her he'd be okay, but it's an Oedipal thing? He's forced to think about something he doesn't want to think about?'

Stephen nodded. 'Yes, that's good. When we have to think about things we don't wish to think about it can tie us up in knots – and, as we all know, sex and parents don't go together, do they? So God knows how we ever got conceived.'

His students smiled uncomfortably. Stephen pictured Audrey in her barbed-wire number, exposing herself in smoke-filled nightclubs, her voice insufficient for the success she craved. And his father, in the shadows at the back of the stage, screened by the piano, watching her, seeing the lecherous faces, hearing the whispered vulgarities.

'But, in a way, that merely describes the problem, it doesn't explain it. After all, if he's feeling that uncomfortable he'd stop thinking about it and just get on with his revenge, his putting things right. So there's more to it than that – there always is, with Shakespeare. So what else is there? Any ideas?'

'What about the politics?'

'What about them, Peter?'

'Well, there's something rotten in the state of Denmark. It's a closed society with a veneer of lawfulness. There's secrecy and suspicion. The production I saw had intelligence men and secret police – that sort of thing. So Hamlet's scared, he must be. He's got to pick his moment.'

'That's a good point. So now we've got two things going: Hamlet's psychological conflict and his positioning within a certain kind of repressive hierarchical society. Remember what we said: psychology and society are always imbricated. Shakespeare is an intensely political playwright as well as a master at depicting individual and family psychology. However, we mustn't get carried away by the secret police – literally or metaphorically. Such things are the director's interpretation –

interpellation – of a subtextual nuance. It's there in the play, but it means different things at different epochs. So what else?'

He watched them all staring into space, glancing at their watches, toying with their mobiles. Somebody sighed.

'Nobody?'

Jack put up his hand, his face pleading to be ignored.

'Yes?'

'Uh ... isn't Shakespeare just telling us something?'

Stephen saw heads turn, glances exchanged. 'Certainly he is. Any idea what?'

'Well ...'

'Yes?'

'I can't explain it very well ...'

Stephen waited. He waited some more, holding his breath, his eyes on Jack, willing him to speak.

Jack looked towards the exit, up at the lights, down at his hands '... Isn't he telling us that Hamlet is a moral agent and the kind of man who instinctively avoids conflict? So, like ...'

'Yes?'

'Well ... like ... he's not a super action hero. He's learned something awful, his world's turned upside down, so he does what most people do – retreats into himself. And ... and he thinks and worries and wonders ... His father's been betrayed and he's been betrayed. He wants to find out more. He wants to know the extent of people's guilt. He wants to see how far they'll go, how many lies they're prepared to tell, how far he can push them before they crack up – before he cracks up. He wants to keep his secret. As long as he keeps his secret then he feels he has a kind of power ... I'm not explaining it very well ...'

'His secret?'

'Yes.'

'What secret, Jack?'

Jack looked at Stephen. 'That he knows what's going on.'

Stephen turns around, his back to the stunned class, watching the dream of a memory.

It is the night of his wedding anniversary. The four of them are seated at their favourite table in the corner, where the lights are low: Stephen opposite Sarah, Paul next to her, Lorna next to Stephen. Conversation has divided, and he finds himself talking to Lorna, shut out by Paul and Sarah, who are sitting back, Sarah leaning towards Paul, one hand in her lap, the other held to her mouth. Lorna is telling Stephen how treasures lost in archives for centuries can suddenly turn up, and then the world has a new symphony by Mozart, a Shakespeare sonnet, or another version of *Metropolis*.

She takes a sip of water, ice cubes jangling. '... Isn't it wonderful, Stephen? The past is buried all around us, only we don't know it. It's as if it's waiting to be discovered. Isn't that fascinating? It only takes someone like me to unearth it, quite by chance.'

Stephen admires her enthusiasm, the way her smile illuminates her face. A quite ordinary face, made attractive by a guileless personality, eager to believe, ready to trust. 'You must live for such a day, Lorna,' he says, after another mouthful of Gevrey Chambertin.

Lorna frowns at him. 'Now you're teasing me! If that was all there was to the job then I'd leave tomorrow. The chances of my discovering something sensational in the county archive are pretty slim.'

'Oh, I don't know. There must be plenty of deep dark secrets ...'

'... next time in Oxford?' mumbles Paul.

'... left behind by all those Victorian patriarchs submerged in their double lives.'

'You'd think so, wouldn't you? But then they'd hardly commit them to paper, would they?'

'No, but others might.' Stephen turns, sees bowed heads, sparkling eyes. 'What are you two talking about so earnestly?'

Paul, abruptly expressionless, reaches for his glass, drinks, drinks again. Sarah, brightly smiling, turns to Lorna. 'Your husband was trying to persuade me to run away with him, Lorna. He says he has a lot of money you don't know about. Kickbacks from road haulage companies desperate for cut-price tyres.'

'Ha!' Paul splutters over his wine. 'Chance would be a fine thing.'

'What would, dear?' asks Lorna. 'The money or Sarah?'

Sarah laughs, smiles conspiratorially at Stephen, who returns her smile, adds a wink. Paul says nothing, slides into monosyllables and too much wine. Stephen begins to worry about him, about Lorna, forgets Oxford, remembers it now, wonders why it cuts at his heart ...

'Professor Ketley?'

Sarah has a conference in Oxford in early January ...

'Professor Ketley? Are you all right?'

Stephen turned and met the collective gaze of his class. He stared at all the young faces. There were so many of them. Where had they come from, where would they go? What lives awaited them they could not know and he could not tell them. He felt sorry for them, suddenly, as if the responsibility and the guilt were all his for what they might find out years hence, when he was gone and forgotten.

He shook his head. 'Sorry! I'm becoming your archetypal absentminded professor. I was just trying to recall that question of Macbeth's about mental illness. Can anyone remind me?'

Jenny sat up, looked quizzical. 'You mean: "Canst thou not minister to a mind diseased, pluck from the memory a rooted sorrow ... er ... raze out the written troubles of the brain and with some sweet oblivious ... antidote ... help! ...'

Stephen helped, joining in on the last line: '... cleanse the stuffed bosom of that perilous stuff which weighs upon the heart?'

Jenny laughed.

'Very good! How come you know all that?'

'It's one of my favourite lines.'

'Mine too! I was wondering how far it could be applied to Hamlet. It's an interesting question ... yes ... a very interesting question ...'

Stephen picked up his notes and rolled them into a tube. A minute to go. He spoke quickly, eager to wrap things up. 'Anyway, someone said something just now. It was Jack. A gift to us all from the gods in the back row.'

Jack looked sheepish, pleased.

'He's made an extremely interesting point. It's one we find difficult to understand these days, when so much emphasis is placed on immediate action. Our society stresses the need to grasp every last shred of life and live it to the full. In practice this often means we're too busy shopping and texting actually to live the lives we have. Speed, you see – speed of reaction, speed of life – does not equate with the experience of life in all its richness and subtlety. Undoubtedly, we have gained an awful lot since

Shakespeare's day, and probably none of us would like to swap our epoch for his. But it's important to realize what we have lost. Perhaps we need to rediscover the rewards of taking our time instead of using it. The advantages of interiority, of reflection. Of self-doubt. Of protecting our privacy. And – as with Hamlet – waiting out our vengeance.'

Stephen watched the clock sweep away the hour's possibilities. 'Thanks for reminding us of that, Jack.' He took a deep breath. 'Time's up! Let's all get out of here and join the land of the living. See you next time.'

The usual noise broke out, chair seats flapping back, the heavy tread of feet on the hollow flooring thudding with dull insistency.

'Oh! The next time you brain yourself on a lamppost because you were too busy looking at your mobile, think of Hamlet, won't you?'

They laughed. Stephen liked to end on a joke.

Then, abruptly, they were gone, all of them. All except Jack. He stood up, put his satchel over his shoulder, looked down at Stephen with those strange green eyes.

Stephen called up. 'Well done! That wasn't so bad, was it? In my opinion, your intervention was the most interesting of the entire class – and that includes my own. Pity we had to wait till the last minute to hear it.'

'I was taking my cue from Hamlet.'

Stephen grinned. 'We'll speak soon. And Jack? Thanks. I really appreciate what you said.'

Stephen headed for his office. Passing a parade of bleary windows, he saw a sullen sky, a stiff wind scolding recalcitrant trees. He whispered as he climbed the stairs. 'Secrets. Sarah and Paul. Me – the biggest secret of all.' He paused to get his breath while he stood before the departmental notice board, his eyes ranging over the announcements and the reminders, seeing nothing – nothing at all.

The toneless clatter of arpeggios on computer keyboards accompanied him along the corridor.

'Stephen!'

He turned, saw Sue Morse through the open door, peering at him over her gold-rimmed glasses. 'Come in, won't you?'

Stephen leant against the lintel, arms full of satchel. 'Shouldn't you be at work?'

Sue swivelled her chair, looked at the clock on her bookcase. 'I've another half hour to while away. While it away with me!'

Stephen admired, as he always did, her vivid shock of ginger hair, the freckles on her nose, the buttoned-down minimalism of her dress and her office. 'My mother always told me to watch out for redheads.'

Sue smiled. 'I can assure you your virtue's safe with me.'

Stephen sighed theatrically. 'Story of my life.' He caught hold of the door and gave her a significant look as – with exaggerated care – he left it ajar. 'Just so we understand one another.'

But Sue was eager for business, he could tell. After the usual polite enquiries, she came straight to the point. 'Let's not beat about the bush,' she advised.

'Let's not.' He sat down, satchel on his lap.

'It's about Gordon. First, we have to arrange a little something for his leaving. Ordinarily, of course, this wouldn't be a problem, but in view of the circumstances – his illness, its possible effects – we need to think carefully. It's no good organizing something that he won't feel able to enter into. And then there's the question of speeches. Should we or shouldn't we? And what should they contain? They can hardly make reference to his retirement into peaceful twilight years.'

'Why not ask him what he wants?'

'I thought of his wife.'

'Anthea? Yes, why not?'

'Would you like to broach the subject? I hardly know her.'

Stephen looked at her, pursed his lips. 'Have you been deputed to take on the arrangements, whatever they turn out to be?'

Sue shrugged and fidgeted with her pen. 'As one of the token women of the department it was thought I would have the necessary emotional empathy and domestic experience.' She laughed silently. 'Clearly, my real qualities – or lack of them – have scarcely impinged on my male colleagues.'

Stephen smiled at Sue's ginger hair. 'In other words, you volunteered.'

Sue stiffened. 'It wasn't quite as straightforward as that.'

'You volunteered.' Stephen shook his head at her. 'You're a scheming minx, Sue, and I can't help admiring you for it. And I can have a word with Anthea, if you like. I don't know her well ...'

'But you do know her, at least.'

'Yes. She always struck me as a rather fragile personality. I hope she'll be able to cope over the coming years. I still haven't taken it in properly, have you?'

'I don't take things in, Stephen. I deal with them with brisk efficiency. It's my way of coping.'

Stephen nodded, wondered what it must be like for Sue's family, living with all that brisk efficiency. 'Second?'

'Second?'

'You prefaced your briskly efficient remarks with the word "First", I recall.'

Sue fidgeted some more with her pen, glanced at her computer, shuffled some papers. She stood up and walked to the window. It was a pleasant view of the campus from her office, surrounded by the ring road and the city suburbs. She stood there with her back to Stephen, silent, shoulders stiff. 'I know every shadow of this view ... every doorway ... every window ... every road. I know which trees will first change their colours ... the direction of the wind blowing across the boating lake ... the way the weather masses on the horizon ... I know when each streetlight will switch on.' She took a deep breath, let it go, turned. 'I know it all and I'm heartily sick of it.'

Stephen, surprised, looked at her serious face looking at him, wondered where this was heading. 'I'll swap you. My view is of the car park. All human life is there, according to George.'

'I presume you know what I'm leading up to.'

Stephen shrugged, crossed his legs. 'Either you want us to run away together to some more agreeable clime, or ... or you wish to talk about Gordon's job.'

Sue returned to her desk, sat down, looked distracted.

'You're not going to rearrange everything again, are you? I think your pen is quite happy where it is.'

Sue smiled. 'No, I'm not. I merely wish to state frankly that I'd like the job.'

'Who wouldn't?'

'George wouldn't.'

'He's told you?'

'He's told everyone.'

Stephen nodded. 'Good old George. I think he's more

interested in doing up his Vanden Plas Austin Princess than he is in professional preferment.'

'I have the impression he's hanging on by his fingernails.'

'I know you've never really liked him, but you could be right. He's difficult to fathom. He comes out with those statements of his and we take them at their face value ...' Stephen sighed, let the words tail off into silence and a vacant stare.

'Yes? Stephen?'

'What?'

'Are you all right? You look odd.'

'So people keep telling me.' Stephen shook himself. 'Anyway, what did you want to know?'

Sue tilted her head, reached for her pen, withdrew her hand when Stephen raised an eyebrow. 'I just wondered about your intentions. Can you tell me?'

'I can't even tell myself.' Stephen stood up, arms around his satchel. He looked at the charging clouds. 'There's a lot going on at the moment – this thing with Gordon's illness, then Christmas and the rest of it – personal stuff. Put it this way: I'd like to be interested in the job and I might have a bash ...'

'Have a bash?'

'... but I just haven't got the time to think about it right now. Does that make sense?'

Sue nodded dubiously but seemed contented. 'I can

commence my campaign untroubled by enemies in the field.'

The war metaphor depressed him. As did Sue's refusal to take the hint he was troubled by something other than his job prospects. He asked himself why it was he felt the need to confide in unsympathetic people.

For lunch, he collected a couple of large hamburgers, two wallets of chips and a large chocolate milkshake from the student's burger bar on campus. He smuggled them into his office and ate greedily and guiltily with his back to the door. The meal became increasingly repellent as he chewed his way through unknown ingredients, but at least it made him feel bloated and substantial. Until, that is, he saw himself in the mirror and watched as his waistband glided over a belly filled with concrete.

That afternoon an idea occurred to him. He phoned his wife's departmental secretary. 'June? Stephen Ketley.'

'Oh, hello! I'm afraid Sarah's not here.'

'Yes, I know. I just wondered if you could tell me the date of her next faculty meeting. I'm trying to arrange something and I don't want it to clash.'

'That should be on Monday as usual ... just a moment ... yes, the fifteenth.'

'That's what I thought, thanks. By the way, was the last meeting also on a Monday?'

'Yes, last week.'

'Not a Friday?'

'Friday? No, definitely Monday.'

'Really? There's no other kind of meeting scheduled for Fridays, is there?'

'No. Fridays are sacrosanct, you know that.'

'That's what I thought. Thank you, June. Oh, and June? Please don't mention I called. It's a surprise.'

'You can rely on me.'

He put down the phone, which rang immediately. 'Hello, Stephen, it's Paul.'

Stephen held his breath, his stomach abruptly at war with undigested burgers and a chocolate milkshake. His body was trembling, the hand that gripped the phone wet with anxiety.

'Sorry I didn't call back sooner. I was away.'

He found himself trusting the voice of his friend even as he told himself those days were over. He thought quickly, his mind ranging over possibilities. It must have been Sarah who'd told Paul to phone, after that conversation they'd had the other day – the other week? – when he'd said how odd it was that Paul had not returned his call. 'Where were you?' he managed to ask.

'Oh – all over the place, you know.'

Not too bright, that, Paul. You have to learn to improvise with conviction. Remember to list the itinerary of your trips – Sheffield, Liverpool, Newcastle – the restaurants and the customers, how the car played up, what the weather was like up North.

'Sell many tyres?' That, after all, is the purpose of your job, that and playing dirty tricks on your wife and best friend. Life without a conscience dogging your footsteps must be rife with possibilities.

'You make it sound like a car boot sale.'

Stephen gazed through the window and saw it was sleeting. Semi-frozen ice was blown horizontal by a fierce wind that had raced in from Sue's horizon, long after his lunchtime quest for burgers and substance.

'You said you wanted to see me,' Paul reminded him, sounding wary, unsure of his welcome.

And what was his welcome? Stephen could not decide – what to say, how to postpone, react, instigate, plot. He wasn't used to this sort of thing, wasn't cut out for it. His safe wholesome world had been blown apart by chance remarks and the sight of his wife in love with another man, bought at the price of a teenager's misery and a bowl of pasta. He should feel anger, rage, the need for exterminating vengeance – not this fearful sadness, this pity for himself and everyone – even Paul.

'It can wait, Paul. I was worried about something, but Sarah reassured me everything was all right.'

Stephen sensed his friend's sigh of relief, the seconds of

elation ticking by in the silence. 'Well, if you're sure.'

'Oh, yes, I'm sure.'

'We'll all be getting together soon, of course.'

'Of course. How's Lorna?'

'Lorna's fine. Looking forward to Christmas.'

'I'm glad someone is.'

Paul chuckled. Too heartily, as if laughing at his jokes could somehow make amends.

Stephen enjoyed the power of his own mercy, of not forcing the issue. Like a Roman emperor feared for his cruelty, he relished confounding expectations and granting clemency by means of an upturned thumb. Only, watch out next time.

'We'll have a long discussion next time we meet, Paul. There's a great deal we need to talk about.'

'Oh?' Pause. 'What about?'

'Sorry! I must go. Got a class. Be seeing you all of a sudden, Paul.'

Stephen hung up, kept his hand on the phone. His heart felt heavy with a complicated and unfathomable pain.

7

Sunday morning. Ten grams lost. Stephen dug out an old pair of braces, his belts now too large to be any use.

Sarah was in the study, grading papers, Emma in her bedroom – 'my Ketley bedroom'. Things had not been good between the two of them. His stepdaughter had arrived three nights ago, fresh from an argument with her father and straight into another one with her mother. According to Emma, Andrew had been in a foul mood for weeks and had been taking it out on her. 'Everything I do is wrong! Just because he's on his own he thinks I have to look after him!'

'On his own? I thought he had another girlfriend.'

'They split up.'

Stephen had immediately felt guilty, as he always did whenever something bad happened to Emma's father. Andrew's rotten luck invariably landed like an accusation. 'Well, he's probably feeling upset, and taking it out on you. I'm sorry.'

Emma and Sarah had been arguing about her future, her sense of purpose, the folly of taking a year off. Nothing came of these disputes except tense silences and vociferous rows, often conducted from opposite ends of the stairs.

Stephen sat at the kitchen table with his laptop, reading an email from Giuliana. The room was warm from cooking, the breakfast dishes stacked by the sink, ready for washing. He stretched, walked to the window, waited for the kettle to boil. Outside, another day of scudding clouds, the sibilant hiss of fractious trees. It looked cold, the deserted streets dripping with winter's spite.

If he craned round hard enough he could just make out the extension where Sarah sat in the study. He watched her working at her desk, turning papers, glancing at her computer. He admired her figure, the way her hair fell, her familiar gestures. It seemed to him that she had hardly changed these last ten years. If anything, maturity had increased her attractiveness. He remembered her passion. How she had loved him! And now this secret life, with its carefully planned deceit and improvised deceptions. Her preoccupation made her look innocent, but she had made a fool of him, as she had of Andrew. He watched her, tried to work himself out of self-pity into some kind of outrage. The kettle boiled.

He made his second cup of coffee, sipped at it, found himself rereading Giuliana's message. It had been months since either of them had written. He could not recall where they had left off, what news had been communicated, withheld. It felt important to keep things light whenever he wrote, and Giuliana, too, sent him guarded messages that spoke to no great purpose, that ended oddly with a cursory sign-off, as if someone unexpected had come into the room.

Today, another short message, this time full of news. 'Ciao Stephen! I'm coming to London! There is the preview of a film we scripted, hosted by the Italian embassy. I can obtain an invitation for you, if you like. I hope so. It's about time you saw something of my work. Besides, you need to hear Italian. You never could speak it like you should. Let me know.'

He imagined her sitting at her computer somewhere in Rome, thinking of him while she found the right words. Her invitation exhilarated him, depressed him. He asked himself if seeing Giuliana was just what he needed or the worst thing he could do, at this time in his marriage, when all seemed over. He thought about it while he finished his coffee, his eyes going over her words, his mind wandering to Christmas, to Audrey's increasing demands for company, for him, for Angela. 'Why can't you get her to come, Stephen? It's not much to ask of my own daughter, is it? And what about Sarah? Surely she can spare some time from that bloody book of hers?'

He put his hand to his stomach. It had that acid feeling that spelled trouble. He couldn't decide what to do, what should happen now, what it was he wanted. Keeping Sarah had been his first impulse, but perhaps he'd already lost her. He knew – could recall – how she committed herself entirely in a new relationship. She'd done it with him, probably with Andrew, so why not with Paul? The difference this time was the betrayal on both sides. Lorna would be devastated.

If Paul were serious about Sarah, then nothing could be done. If it meant little to him – if he had simply grabbed the chance for a free bit of pink – then it could all end soon, no matter what Sarah felt. But then, would she return to her husband? And would he want her? Betrayal is a complex business. It wasn't just a momentary step out of line and then back on track.

Stephen stood at the sink, emptied the coffee grounds, washed the glassware and the crockery, his eyes fixed beyond the misted window pane, beyond the fence to the garden, beyond this life suddenly so febrile.

'There is always a snake in the garden,' he whispers.

He finds a bench, closes his eyes for a moment's respite from the sun's glare, feels cradled in its heat. Santa Croce towers mythically, unreal, a shimmering phantasm, despite the sounds of the city, the people with cameras and ice creams, his own tour of the chapels and frescoes, where the hallowed light washes over his astonished gaze. Each day he asks if the marvels of Florence will end, whether he will grow tired suddenly with so much beauty, the dazzling weight of history. The city tells him no, its charm unending, unbreakable. He fills his lungs with the warm air rising from the flagstones; life, too, feels inexhaustible at this moment, with every sunrise another promise, and all of them kept.

Giuliana, dressed in white, stands on the steps to the basilica, searching for her sunglasses in the straw bag she carries over her shoulder. She seems to Stephen like a bright and singular angel of purity against all those dark steps worn down by centuries of glory and corruption – he knows he has been admiring too many Fra Angelicos. She looks for him, and he imagines her eyes seeking him out behind those inscrutable lenses. She sees him, waves; he returns her wave, smiles with the pleasure of her recognition. He watches her come to him, cutting a joyous diagonal across the piazza, lightly lightly tripping, skirt swaying, hair floating. A deep melancholy fills his heart. It is too much for him to bear, all this happiness, yet still not enough, not nearly so.

And then the snake. Stephen watches, sees the young man in jeans and open-neck shirt, obviously Florentine. Not English, anyway – no Englishman can look like that. Ease and confidence, immediate familiarity, at home in body and mind – these are Latin accomplishments. His mouth is the shape of mischief and cruelty, his eyes know things. He accosts Giuliana, who greets him familiarly, warmly, and they talk and laugh while Stephen looks on, resentful, suddenly bitter. They make some arrangement – there is much looking at watches, pointings east and west – and they say goodbye, amid smiles and waves and backward glances.

'Who was that?' asks Stephen, watching the man safely out of sight.

'Tonio. A friend. I didn't know he was back.'

'Back?'

'He's been living in Rome these past months. Where shall we go now?'

'Is he in love with you?'

Giuliana laughs. 'Maybe. I don't know.'

'Are you meeting him somewhere?'

'Perhaps. Why?'

'Alone?'

'That depends.'

'On what?'

Giuliana looks at him. 'On other people. Why are you asking all these questions?'

Feelings he cannot understand and must not trust prevent him from telling her the truth. His jealousy feels petty, unreasonable. He has no claim on Giuliana and, even if he has, it can only be partial, while they wait out the summer, when he will leave her to her life. For he has to go back. It is hard to live in a strange place. They have no words there for how he feels.

A cat tiptoed along the back fence. Stephen watched it until, suddenly, it was gone, as if it was never there. Somewhere, he could hear voices. Sarah was on the prowl. A door slammed, a stifled cry. Shouting now, muffled rage. He heard heavy footsteps on the floor above.

He walked to the sitting room and searched in the bookcase for his published PhD thesis. *Wharton, Ruskin and the American Impressionists in Florence* was dedicated to Giuliana, 'who showed me how to love Italian style'. The ambiguity had been deliberate. He wondered now why he had been so circumspect. He had never sent her a copy.

He sat with the book in his lap, hands clutching at the arms of his chair. Sunday morning was his time for deciding what to do, and in what order. So much of it involved women. The thought surprised him. He had to make another try with his sister. He had to see Anthea Zellaby. He had to talk to Sarah. It didn't feel as if he were ready for any of it.

More noise – Sarah and Emma were still going at it. Another exclamation shrieked and echoed, then Emma was thundering down the stairs, searching him out. 'I'm out of here! Now! I can't stand her another minute!' Arms crossed, she stood at the window, glaring at injustice.

'What happened? Everything was all right a minute ago.'

'She said I was making too much noise and she couldn't concentrate – God knows how, because I had on my headphones

...'

'Well, they do leak and you have the volume up really high.'

'... and then she started again – again! – wittering on about university and what I should and shouldn't do, and taking off a year was a stupid idea, and so was engineering ... I thought you said she'd be pleased?'

'Did I? I thought she'd come round to the idea ...'

'She won't ever come round to anything unless it's what she wants!'

'Give it time, Emma. These things always work themselves out.'

'Tell her that!'

'Tell her what?' Startled, they both turned and saw Sarah on the threshold.

'I'm leaving!' Emma repeated.

'Fine! Where will you go? You've just come from your father.'

'Anywhere's better than here!'

Stephen got to his feet, his book pressed to his chest. 'Look, you two, let's calm down! Emma! It really isn't a good idea to shuttle between your parents every time there's a disagreement. We all have to learn to face things, not run away.'

'Tell her that!'

Sarah put her hands on her hips. 'I'm not the one who's running out.'

'Then stop trying to run my life! I can make up my own mind what I want to do. I don't need you to tell me I'm wrong.'

'Someone's got to! It's obvious you don't know what you're doing, and all your father does is meddle.'

'That's all you both do – meddle! Stop using me to get back at him. I don't know why you still hate him after all this time.'

'I don't – '

'What's wrong, a guilty conscience?'

There was a moment's pause. Stephen looked at Emma, saw her take a step away from her mother.

Sarah was shaking. 'How dare you speak to me in that manner! You want to go, so go! Get out of this house! Now, right now!'

Stephen moved between them. 'Sarah – '

'Will you kindly go! Now! This minute!'

'Stop it! Both of you!'

He could hear their breathing above the gurgling of the radiator beneath the window. Another gust of wind sent the old plane tree on the pavement into a frenzied clamour. Somebody walked by the house, her head bowed against the furious air tugging at her coat.

Stephen turned to Emma. 'I'd like to talk to your mother. You go to your room and calm down.'

'She started it!'

'Emma!'

He closed the door after her, turned to Sarah. 'This can't go on.'

'Tell her that! Tell Andrew!'

'I'm telling you. Sit down, won't you? We need to talk.'

'What about?'

'Let's sit down.'

'I need to get back to work.'

'In a minute.'

He sat on the sofa, while she hesitated, chose a chair opposite, across the coffee table. He watched her run a hand through her hair, noted the familiar fall of the longer strands as they slipped over her ear. She looked tired, her face tense from work, her mouth set tight, resolved to secrecy. Even her clothes looked reticent, greys and browns like a winter landscape, fallow for the future.

Sarah is weak. The thought occurred to him gradually; he could not say how or why. Her posture, perhaps – that listless slump, shoulders down, eyes on her hands clasped in her lap – or the exchange of energy between the two of them as they faced one another, uncertain how to begin, fearful where it might end. And with the thought that she was weak – believed herself to be weak – it was like she really knew nothing – nothing – as long as he knew something. It was as if she and Paul held no secrets, none at all, and that it was he who held a secret; *he* whose knowledge was dangerous. He marvelled at the idea. He could preserve his pride and his dignity. Something akin to elation swept over the surface of his skin.

'You've got to stop treating Emma like disputed territory to be fought over in a war between you and Andrew. She's a person in her own right.'

Sarah raised her eyes, looked at him, expressionless. 'As long as she's dependent on me – us – then I have to defend her interests. Andrew is the one at fault. He can't let go.'

'You don't know that! If Emma decided to study art history or literature you wouldn't think twice. Just because she's thinking of following her father's path you think she's being got at. Can't you see the inconsistency in that?'

'It's not a question of consistency, it's authenticity. What Emma does now will decide what she is for the rest of her life. She can't be allowed to make a serious error. She's still a child.'

'Then surely it's all the more commendable of her to want to take a year off. If she's unsure what she wants to do, why not look upon that as a good sign? It means she won't be pushed around by Andrew.'

Sarah grew impatient. 'Apart from the fact that a year off at this stage is a stupid idea, I know Andrew. He will do his utmost to convince her of what he wants. And what he wants is to get back at me. At us.'

'You don't think you're being a touch paranoid about Andrew? You've barely met him for a decade. You don't know him any better than I do – not any more.'

'I know what he's like. It's quite obvious from what Emma lets slip that he still blames me for what happened. I'm only trying to do what's right, but he won't let me. And neither, it seems, will you.'

Stephen paused. 'You want to do what's right, do you?'

'Yes, of course ...'

In the silence that followed, when their eyes met, it felt to Stephen as if, for one brief moment, they had stepped to the brink of comprehending what the other knew but could not say. It seemed to frighten them both.

'Look, Sarah, this isn't a cold war we're fighting here, talking about Emma in lieu of something else that frightens us much too much to face. I want to do right by Emma – '

'And I don't, I suppose?'

'Of course you do. But doing right by her means allowing her to decide for herself. And supporting her in whatever she does decide. She's not a child – not completely, anyway. She's also a young woman with a mind of her own.'

'A mind still pushed this way and that by you and Andrew.'

'Now you're being unfair. I'm not pushing her to do anything in particular. Just to be herself. That's difficult enough.'

'You *would* take her side. You always have. You've always come between us.'

Stephen, astonished, watched resentment take hold of her face. 'That's not true! Remember, I also had a hand in bringing her up. It wasn't all her natural parents – sometimes it felt like it wasn't them at all. I've given you all the support I could. I've looked after her when you were away, I've always been pleased to ferry her around and keep her from disturbing you. It's tough caught between you and Andrew – tough for me and tough for Emma.'

'And so I'm to blame, am I? For working hard, for giving her a home? My God! First Andrew, now you!'

'Will you forget about Andrew? I'm beginning to think Emma was right – you do have a guilty conscience! You're always the victim, no matter what you do. I see now why you don't get on with Audrey. She's too similar. You're two of a kind, you and she.'

'And I'm beginning to think you're more in love with Emma than you are with me!'

'That's disgusting! I love her like a daughter. Which is what she is, in a way.'

'Perhaps I'm wrong. Perhaps it's that Italian bit you really love.'

'And who do you love, Sarah? Answer me that.'

Sarah's mouth opened and closed. She stood up. 'There's clearly no point in continuing this conversation until you've calmed down.'

'Until *I've* calmed down!'

'I need to get back to work.'

'Still much to do, is there?'

Sarah, hand on the doorknob, looked back at him. 'Yes.' Her voice sounded hoarse.

'I expect you're looking forward to tackling the final chapter one day.'

'One day.'

They looked at one another, Stephen holding her gaze until Sarah's eyes dropped. She opened the door and left the room.

In the minutes that followed, while he thought about what had been said, Stephen decided to accept Giuliana's invitation. It could do no harm.

He stood up, paced around, found himself still holding his book. He shoved it back on the shelf, put his hands in his pockets, checked his watch. He couldn't leave Emma alone in her room, wondering.

Stephen knocked at Emma's door. 'It's me. May I come in?' He looked at the sign, *Emma's Room*, stencilled in red from when she was a child, and wondered if she'd heard. Then she was standing there, stepping aside for him to enter. He wondered if she'd been crying; thought not.

Her room was characteristically tidy, books arranged flush to their shelves, items on the desk stacked in neat parallels. She would make a good engineer. He sat at her desk, embarrassed as always by his presence in her inner sanctum, unable to sit on the bed, eager to be brief. Sarah's absurd accusation – had she meant it? – knocked at his head. He knew it wasn't true. His feelings for Emma were entirely legitimate. The baser instincts that lurked around the corner were, he guessed, quite normal in their way. A good and balanced individual recognizes them and leaves them alone.

She sat on the bed, oblivious to his turmoil, brooding.

'I hate rows, don't you?'

She nodded, picking at her fingernails, hair screening the side of her face.

Stephen sighed, remembered. 'I saw what they did to my father. You might not think it now, but Audrey was plunged into depression and alcohol after Angela was born. She had these ... explosive eruptions of rage and jealousy. She would brood for days, nursing a drink and a grudge against everyone ... for me because I couldn't understand her pain ... for Angela because she had ended her career ... for my father because it was all his fault – for reasons I could never fathom. She says he made her keep Angela, but how he could have done that really, I don't know. If

Audrey really didn't want to keep the baby, nobody could have stopped her from getting rid of it ... Maybe it was her own weakness she despised.'

The silence pooled between them. Emma did not look up. She spoke, quietly. 'I don't have any idea about your dad.'

'He was a complicated man. Assertive in some ways, meek in others. He was a pushover for Audrey. He was logical, methodical – everything she isn't. I suppose that was the musician in him. He always encouraged me to learn, be inquisitive. I'm grateful for that.'

Emma looked up. 'How was he with Angela?'

Stephen shrugged. 'The same. Then, somehow, all three of them fell out with one another. Angela went off the rails – was never on them.' He stood up, looked, unseeing, through the window to the garden. 'I really don't know anymore. Every family has its own mythology – the story it peddles to keep itself from looking at reality. Angela was our designated black sheep. She had no choice in the matter and couldn't make any of us see differently.'

'That's how I feel.'

'I'm very sorry. You're caught in the middle of us all. I don't know what to advise. Stand your ground and try to rise above it. How does that sound?'

'Easier said than done.'

They both smiled.

'Your mother acts on instinct. She has a brain like a laser beam for her work, but in her private life ... well ... if she sees something, she goes for it.'

Emma nodded. He had the feeling they'd both thought of the same thing.

8

Gordon Zellaby had not yet seriously malfunctioned, as he put it, and was midway through recording some lectures while he still could. Stephen admired his courage, wondering each time they met how long he could postpone the inevitable.

'The inevitable could be interminable,' was Gordon's riposte to Stephen's latest polite enquiry. 'I look to the future with joyous expectation, although I may not be in a fit state to experience it. In the meantime, I've still got some books in me I'd like to write. I hope to bore posterity with them long after I'm out of reach of the critics.' He'd looked at Stephen with something close to commiseration. 'The Zellaby name will live forever. Poor Stephen!'

Stephen wondered what he meant.

Anthea Zellaby had eventually returned Stephen's phone call and invited him round to discuss her husband's leavetaking. 'I can't abide the telephone,' she told him, in clipped crisp tones. 'It's the work of the Devil.'

Stephen shuffled some work about and asked George to take a class while he visited Anthea one morning. He had weighed himself and was contemplating the loss of another few hundred grams, his footsteps slapping soggily over the leaf-covered pavements that led to the Zellaby residence.

Gordon and Anthea had long been comfortably installed in a plush Victorian semi in a desirable neighbourhood. The wooden floors and sash windows, the marble fireplace and the high ceilings accorded well with the deep lumpy sofas with musty cushions, the mysterious bric-a-brac – among other things, Gordon collected Turkish copperware – and the books shelved and stacked in neat piles along the skirting boards. Stephen admired the silent empty rooms as Anthea led him to the kitchen – a big and battered affair with a big and battered dining table, at which they sat. Through the window he saw trees, a pond, a lawn strewn with dead leaves.

Over coffee and Anthea's homemade ginger nuts, Stephen tried to talk about Gordon, but the pro vice-chancellor's serious illness and sudden resignation felt remote from all this ease and comfort. Nothing bad, it seemed, could ever happen in this house.

Anthea laid down topics of conversation like sheets of ice on a frozen road.

'I really don't understand it, do you?' She took another biscuit, pushing the plate nearer to Stephen. 'I mean, phones, as we knew them – Gordon and I – were judged at best as a necessary evil and at worst as an infernal nuisance. Either way they were best avoided. Now they've become essential adjuncts to every conceivable activity. They're worse than cars. Oh! Do you recall what Patrick Hamilton said about the motor car? He said they were like an infestation of beetles, smothering the face of the planet. What would he have said about phones, I wonder? What do you think of these ginger nuts? A bit too ginger?'

Stephen kept up with her as best he could.

'Fragile' had been the wrong word to apply to Anthea. 'Brittle' was closer to the mark, he now realized, biting into another biscuit. Fifteen years Gordon's junior, she had the bright skin-deep sentiments acquired from an upper-class family devoid of profound feelings about everything except gymkhanas and gin and tonics. That, at any rate, was Stephen's conviction. It was a prejudice of his own with no evidential support, but civilization is built on prejudice, as he had often told George. Gordon had married his lean and angular student long before Stephen's time, when the fuss and the scandal had blown over, but each time Stephen met her, he was, despite himself, surprised by her relative youth, her aggressive gentility and her apparent lack of occupation. He looked at her hard eyes and wondered if the Zellabys had been happy together. He supposed they must have been.

As Anthea flitted from one subject to the next, never settling, he asked himself how on earth this woman would cope with a husband losing his mind. Would she even notice? Perhaps she'd be terrific, despite an emotional coldness that made him shiver. Her manner, her ways of speaking, her cool evaluating gaze, surely offered no purchase for anyone's sympathy, least of all her own.

Stephen smiled, glanced at his watch. 'I'm afraid I need to get back quite soon. Do you mind – '

'Of course not! You're here to talk about Gordon's farewells, aren't you?'

'Yes.'

'It's really very good of you all. Gordon will be delighted.'

Stephen couldn't picture Gordon delighted about anything in the circumstances. 'I understand he's asked his PVC colleagues not to do anything at all. However, we were wondering if a quiet low-key event might be appropriate for the department. After all, that's where he's made his academic reputation, and that of the university. Naturally, we don't want to do anything ... er ... inappropriate for him at this time. On the other hand, we'd love to do something, as we all feel so much for him. But, of course, it's entirely up to him.'

'It's terribly sweet of you all. I'm sure Gordon would enjoy something along those lines. After all, he can't simply slope off as if he were in disgrace, can he?'

'No ... Quite. We had in mind a gathering in the common room, for example, with drinks and canapés – that sort of thing.'

'Sounds quite charming.'

'I'm sure you'd like to talk to Gordon about it. Once you know his ... er ... mind, let us know what you'd prefer. There's also the question of speeches. We thought a simple address, a gift of some sort, then leave it at that. If you or Gordon feels up to responding, that would be most welcome.'

'I'll discuss it with Gordon.'

Anthea poured them more coffee, despite Stephen's protestations. 'You can stay a minute more, can't you?' She did not wait for his reply. 'I'm not convinced by these ginger nuts. Try these lemon cookies. They really are delicious. I gather you're a contender, Stephen.'

Stephen took a cookie, said they were rather nice, crumbs cascading to the table. 'A contender for what?'

'PVC. I'm sure you'd be very good at it. So is Gordon.'

'It's kind of you to say so. I –'

'But you need to watch out. Sue Morse is busy making herself indispensable. Minds have yet to be made up on Gordon's successor. Don't let her make them up for you.'

'I've been thinking about it.'

'Gordon will put in a word for you.'

'Yes, he did mention that.'

'You'd be excellent in the job.'

Stephen looked at Anthea as she brushed crumbs from her

cardigan. Asking what lay behind her sudden interest in his career would be a bootless question, but he asked it anyway.

'I want the right man to win,' she told him.

'And you're convinced, are you, that I am the right man?'

'Sue Morse must be stopped. You're the man to do it.'

'What do you have against Sue Morse? She might be excellent in the role.'

Anthea ignored that question. 'Do you want the job?'

Stephen sighed, finished his coffee. 'I don't know. It's awfully hard work and long hours. The pay is good, of course; not to mention the pension ...'

'You're a poet, Stephen!'

'But ... I don't know.'

'Act as if you want it and you will want it. Begin now. Before it's too late. You're good at impressing people – the cocktail circuit. Charm them, Stephen. As you used to charm everyone. How is Sarah?'

Stephen recalled how Anthea would watch from the sidelines as he and Sarah grew closer together and, doubtless, could no longer hide their mutual attraction. It seemed as if he had only to raise his eyes to a far corner of a crowded common room to find Anthea gazing at them with that blank stare of hers that signified intensely dispassionate curiosity. She would glance away as soon as her stare was returned, or else pick up conversation with someone like George, who found her amusing and bizarre – for him, a perfect combination.

He told her that Sarah was fine and now he really had to go.

'You must come round some time. Both of you. Did you have an umbrella?'

'No. Is it raining?'

'It will.'

He looked at the surging clouds from the shelter of the porch. The weather would turn against him, he could tell. A car pulled up behind the hedge to the front garden.

'Good heavens! It's George!' Anthea glanced at Stephen. 'Rather, isn't that George Ringer? He drives one of those old cars, doesn't he?'

Stephen watched George step around the vehicle and open the passenger door. He saw Gordon get out, a little unsteady, a little confused, looking about, looking tired. George helped him through the front gate, Gordon protesting. 'I'm all right! I'm all right! There's no need for all this fuss!'

Gordon seemed suddenly to have aged ten years. His face looked curiously sagged, his body depleted. Instinctively, Stephen held a hand to his own stomach, felt the irritating flap of his gaping waistband.

George held Gordon's elbow as he escorted him to the front door. 'Morning, Mrs Zellaby; morning, Stephen. I've just brought

Gordon home for a rest.'

Gordon stumbled over the doorstep, George behind him. 'Perhaps I could lay down for a minute.' His words came out in little gasps, as if he'd run out of puff.

Anthea asked what was wrong. George whispered he'd tell her later. 'Where should I put him?'

'In the bedroom.'

Stephen watched the three of them climb the stairs, saw George lead the way to a door overlooking the hall. A minute later, George came down. He gave Stephen an awkward smile. 'Gordon dried up recording a lecture for posterity. One minute he was in full flow, the next ...' George snapped his fingers, pulled a face. 'It was a great shock. We thought we should bring him home. He didn't seem to know where he was for a while there. Not even *who* he was. Imagine how that must feel.'

Stephen looked up at the bedroom door, now closed, shook his head. 'I was here about the leaving do, asking what they wanted. It feels pointless now.'

George, dabbing his forehead with a handkerchief, shuffled from one foot to the other. 'Not necessarily. These things will come and go, apparently. On the way here he seemed his old self. Tired, but all right.'

Anthea returned, her face a mask. 'I've left him to sleep. Thank you so much for bringing him home.'

Stephen said goodbye, waited for George on the pavement by the car. The wind got up, the trees shook, raindrops clattered like hail on the roof of the Princess. Stephen watched the two of them talking, Anthea's lips barely moving as she spoke at length, occasionally glancing towards him. George nodded, looked self-conscious, stepping back when Anthea leaned towards him. They exchanged a look that Stephen could not interpret, then shook hands.

George offered him a lift.

Stephen admired the leather upholstery, the walnut and chrome of the Princess, which hummed quietly to the main road. George drove carefully, every gesture economical, every manoeuvre signalled, precise.

'I didn't know you'd still be there,' George told him, lights on red. 'She's a funny one, don't you think?'

'I don't know what to make of her. Is she real? Does she feel? I never know where her manner ends and her real self begins. Assuming she has one.'

George chuckled. 'That's it, exactly.'

'You always liked her, I remember.'

George demurred. 'She's amusing, though. And deeper than you think. I can see what Gordon must have seen in her.'

'I can't see it myself.'

'Of course not, Stephen. You're young, you have your whole

life ahead of you ...'

'You're only three years older than me, George.'

'Three vital years! They make all the difference.'

'If you say so. Hey! Where are you taking us? This isn't the way back.'

'It's lunchtime, Stephen. More or less. I'm taking us to the Kean's Head, for a well-earned pint.'

George bought the drinks.

'Cheers, George.' Stephen sipped his beer with a good conscience, thought how it would give him some weight, build him up.

George, experienced with beer, swallowed great mouthfuls of a dark and menacing bitter, his eyes fixed on the ceiling, head tilted back, glass clicking against his teeth. He gave a satisfied smack of his lips, looked at Stephen. 'Have you heard?'

'Heard what?'

'Sue Morse had the vice-chancellor to dinner a couple of nights ago.'

'Of the exchequer or the university?'

'This is no time for levity, Stephen. She's beating you at your own game. If you don't act fast the job will be hers.'

'Who says? Since when does anything we do change someone's opinion on who they want for the job? We both know the post won't be advertised. They've probably already made up their minds.'

George looked at him in astonishment. 'Are you deliberately being obtuse? Remember, Gordon's resignation was entirely unexpected. No one's made up their mind about anything. They're thinking and looking around. All they can see is Ginger. What are you going to do about it?'

'Why should I do anything about it?'

'Stephen, you could stop Sue in her tracks, if only you'd make the effort.'

'And have vice-chancellors around for dinner every night? No thanks. Life's too short.'

'Don't you even care? Don't you want the job?'

'I'm not sure that I do. Take that as an answer to both your questions.'

'Stephen, you amaze me! You don't have a clue what's going on.'

'There's nothing going on. Is there?'

'For God's sake, open your eyes! You can't afford to be so complacent. Sue Morse, bless her, would be a disastrous PVC. She's like someone out of *The History Man*.'

'*Lucky Jim* more like.'

'Either way, she's bad news.'

'You don't know that. She might be very good.'

George downed the remains of his beer, glanced at Stephen's

glass, half-empty. 'She'd take things in entirely the wrong direction. Before you know it, we'd be forced to take no-talent crowd-pleasing hacks like Sibella Chamberlain seriously. Is that what you want? Can't you see what's at stake here?'

'But why me? If you're so worried why don't you do something about it?'

George held a hand to his mouth, belched, coughed. 'I am doing something about it! I'm asking the man with the best chance of getting the job to exercise himself a little – to care enough, Stephen – to step into the breach.'

'I'll think it over.'

'The time for thinking is over! You need to get going.'

Stephen stared at George. He felt hot suddenly, despite the cool beer wallowing uncomfortably in his empty stomach. He fished a handkerchief from his pocket and dabbed at his face. Beyond the skylight above their corner table, turbulent clouds raced the wind.

'What's wrong?'

Stephen shrugged. 'Oh, I don't know. I'm just a little depressed, I suppose.'

'Depressed? What about?'

'Everything! This business. I wonder what the hell we're all doing, I really do. Don't you?'

George looked blank. 'What do you mean?'

'I mean, here we are studying and expounding on the sublime achievements of English literature, yet we still talk in terms of enemies and battles. Don't you find that depressing? No wonder academics can be such warmongers. They can celebrate the humanity of Shakespeare's *oeuvre* with one part of their brains and advocate the extermination of an entire people with another.'

'But we're not asking you to exterminate an entire people!'

'We?'

George looked sheepish. 'I've been asking around, canvassing opinion – a sweepstake kind of thing.'

'George! Without asking me?'

'I thought I could count on you. What can I say?'

'Honestly, George! I've enough on my plate as it is without you turning against me as well!'

'What the hell are you talking about? I'm on your side, dear boy, if only you knew it. Fancy another?'

George was clearly set on another drink, so Stephen told him yes. 'I'll get them. Same again?'

George nodded, looked at him in puzzlement. 'What exactly is wrong with you, Stephen?' he asked, after he'd started on his second pint. 'And don't tell me it's your weight or this business with Gordon. There's something else, I can tell.'

Stephen decided he needed a friend. If it wasn't George, he could only think of his sister who hated him. 'Sarah and I are ...

well, we're having problems.'

George put down his glass, his mouth agape. 'You are?'

'This is strictly between you and me, George.'

'Of course, dear boy.'

'I don't want to hear you've been canvassing opinion about this as well, okay?'

George nodded, emphatic. 'But what's the problem, if I may ask?'

'I found out ... I found out she's seeing someone else.'

George gasped. 'Are you sure? There's no doubt?'

'None whatsoever.'

At the bar, someone laughed. George stared at the remains of his beer. 'What are you going to do?'

Stephen shook his head. 'I don't know.'

'Does she know you know?'

'More or less.'

'What's that supposed to mean? Either she does or she doesn't.'

'I've dropped hints. That's all I can do at this stage.'

George opened his mouth, said nothing. He watched Stephen for a long moment. 'Who is it?'

'A friend of ours. Married too.'

'The bastard! Tell his wife.'

'Think so?'

'No doubt about it! See how he likes it!'

'Trouble is, she's so very nice and so vulnerable. She'd be devastated, I can tell.'

'No one can tell anything about people in this situation. You thought you knew your wife, you thought you knew your friend. You don't. Tell his wife.'

'I'll think about it. You could be right.'

'Stop thinking, Stephen! Now is the time for action. About everything.' George looked at his watch. 'We'd better get going. She can't do over forty.'

'Who can't?'

'The Princess.'

Stephen had given George to understand that he had – kind of – semi-confronted Sarah with his knowledge of her betrayal. To have admitted the truth felt like a humiliation. George would not have understood. Stephen did not understand.

He phoned his sister repeatedly. She was unavailable, tied up, elsewhere. When they finally spoke, it took him an hour to persuade her to meet again.

They saw one another one evening on neutral ground, at the restaurant where he and Jack had lunched. The place was quiet, the staff attentive. While he waited for Angela to arrive, Stephen drank water, ate olives and thought about his life. There was, he realized, no need any longer to wonder what was wrong.

Everything was wrong. Images of Sarah and Paul in bed together tormented him. The sudden instability of his own position – seemingly so secure, so settled – appalled him. His indecision ... not even that, his inability even to think about deciding what to do – puzzled him. He was afraid of the future.

And now here was his sister, replete with her own troubles and resentments, suspicious of him and his motives, whom he had to convince to visit their mother at Christmas.

Angela sighed, dallied with her coffee spoon. He had waited until they'd finished eating and drinking before broaching the difficult stuff. A good meal, he hoped, would relax them both, make them feel at ease with one another.

'I think you should know that Audrey also wants to see you badly. She asked me to give you this.'

Angela took hold of the envelope, placed it on the table.

'Aren't you going to open it?'

'What is it?'

'A personal invitation. For you and Buzz. Written by Audrey at her own initiative.'

Angela came close to a sneer. 'Is this when I'm supposed to break down and cry? The wayward daughter repents and begs for forgiveness?'

Stephen shook his head. 'Nothing like that. I'd certainly enjoy your company.'

'And Buzz's?'

'He'd also be very welcome. If he has the time.'

Angela bridled. 'It's cracks like that –'

'I didn't mean anything by it! I know he performs around the country. I don't know his commitments, do I?'

Angela looked suspicious, calmed down.

Stephen tried again. 'I can't pretend that Christmas back at the old hacienda will be a barrel of laughs. Audrey will be there, for a start, and there's bound to be rows. But that's what Christmas is about, falling out with your family. Besides, I could use your moral support. It's hard to deal with her on one's own – as you well know.'

'I'll think about it.'

'Will Buzz be free?'

'I don't know, I'll talk to him. Look, I can't really tell you I'm happy about this. My life's moved on from all this stuff. I don't have to make it better.'

'I'd really be grateful if you'd consider it.'

Angela frowned, looked at him. 'Why should you care, Stephen? I mean, what's it to you all of a sudden? It's been like this all our lives, now suddenly it has to be different?'

'I'd like us to get to know one another again, Angela. If you want to, that is.'

'It can't be like before, Stephen.'

'No. I realize that. I thought Christmas would be a good time to start.'

'You don't know half of what went on in that house. It seemed to me you didn't want to know. That's what hurt.'

'I was ... I am aware of how unfairly you've been treated.'

'And I wish you weren't so calm about it. That's another thing. You've got to learn how to feel.'

'I've been learning a lot about that lately.'

Angela said nothing.

At least they had managed to talk about Christmas. At least she'd told him she'd think about it.

When he returned home, Stephen found a note from Sarah. 'Francesca phoned. She's upset. Am visiting. Back tomorrow.'

Francesca was Sarah's dearest friend. She lived in Oxford.

9

‘Next time in Oxford,’ Paul had whispered.

Stephen dialled Sarah’s mobile while he paced through the silent rooms of the empty house, his slippers clattering on the bare boards between the carpets. His home felt cold and unfamiliar, made strange by suspicion and the lateness of the hour.

Number unobtainable.

He found himself in the study, sitting at the desk in Sarah’s chair with its cushion for her back, his eyes on the rug stained years ago by Emma’s chocolate ice cream. Emma was at her father’s, or so she’d said. Outside the uncurtained window, a car rushed by, and the sound was like a cold hand searching for his heart.

He tried Sarah’s number again and again, over many minutes, his fingers stiff with the repetition, pained by their rigid grasp of the phone. His mind wandered. While Away the Loneliness, Audrey’s signature tune, came into his head, his mother singing his father’s composition with that plaintive murmur she had made her own.

And I wait for you each lonely night …

Yet it was she for whom they'd waited, he and his father, when Dad had slowed down on the performing, desperate to write more hit songs. All those days and nights with Audrey gone, when the rhythm of their lives pulsed evenly without her, peacefully, to be blasted by her sudden arrival, blazing with frenzy and tension, her mood high from her latest performance, her kisses and cuddles full of cigarette smoke, bestowed distractedly, impatiently, for she was eager to be gone, back on the road ...

... And it feels like you've always been gone ...

Stephen shook the melody from his head. The phone rang. Scrambling to pick it up, he watched it spin out of his hand and fall to the floor. He bent down, struck his head on the desk, bit his tongue. His temper flared. 'Sarah!'

'It's me, Stephen. Lorna.'

Stephen was rubbing the pain from his head. 'What?'

'Lorna.'

'Oh! Hello, Lorna.'

'Are you all right?'

'Yes ... yes. I dropped the phone and hit my head.'

'Oh.' It was a distracted exclamation, made by a tired mind. 'I'm ... I'm so sorry to ring you at this late hour.'

'That's all right ... Is it late?'

'I wondered if you could come over. First thing tomorrow, I

mean.'

'Is something the matter?'

'Can you come?'

'Of course. Is ... is Paul there?'

'No. I'll see you tomorrow.'

A click and she was gone. Stephen looked at the phone, thought of the cat he'd seen disappearing like a dream over the garden fence. His head still hurt. He checked for blood, found none. He'd have to remember not to drag a comb over it tomorrow.

He needed a drink. He thought there were some beers somewhere in the kitchen. He dug them out and sat at the table, opening the bottles one by one, pouring bitter into his glass, pressed down to overflowing, the drone of the fridge for accompaniment. Number still bloody unobtainable. He needed to talk to someone. All he could think of was George.

'Hello?'

George was hoarse and irascible. Stephen pictured him in bed, hair tousled, a hangover gnawing at his throat. 'Sorry to wake you, George.'

'Stephen? Good God! What time is it?'

'I don't know. Late.' There were muffled sounds at George's end, whisperings. 'Can you talk?'

George told him to wait. Stephen opened another beer, the

bottle top rattling on the table, clinking to the floor. There was a confused scrambling noise in his ear, then the sound of a closing door.

'What is it?' asked George, breathless.

'I'm all alone in the house. I'm drinking beer in the kitchen. Sarah is in Oxford. I think she's with *him*. His wife called. I'll be seeing her tomorrow.'

George yawned. 'Does she know?'

'I don't know.'

'Will you tell her?'

'I don't know.'

'Well, what do you want me to do?'

'I needed someone to talk to. When life disintegrates one needs a friend.'

George sighed, quoted Yeats. 'Things fall apart, the centre cannot hold ...'

'Ever asked yourself why the bloody hell not?'

'W. B. didn't get around to that.'

Stephen hiccoughed. 'You're not much use to me, are you, George?'

'Nobody can help you except yourself, Stephen.'

'You should be asking me how I'm feeling, stuff like that.'

'How are you feeling?'

'I don't know. Angry. Hurt. Drunk. This must be what they

call a dark night of the soul.'

George sighed again. 'You're so unresisting, Stephen. It makes me furious. If you don't put up some resistance to what life throws at you, then you lose yourself. You give in to everything and everyone.'

There was a long silence while Stephen supped some beer and George said nothing. 'Are you listening?' George asked.

'Yes, I'm listening.'

'It's the same with the job. You're going to let someone snatch it from you simply because you can't bring yourself to act. I don't know what's happened to you. Do you?'

'No. I don't.' Stephen looked at his hand on the table, like a lobster's claw around his empty glass.

'Are you still there?'

Stephen shook himself awake. 'You've been grand, George. Get back to bed. Sorry to have disturbed you.'

'Stephen –'

'Goodnight, George.' He hung up.

Snakes and secrets ... He wondered who George had in bed. No, he didn't want to know. Had his friend diagnosed correctly? He asked himself if he was really unable to resist what life threw at him – Audrey, Sarah, work. He had resisted Giuliana all right.

He tried the phone. Number unobtainable. He drank some more, found himself at his computer, writing out his pain –

writing a letter to Giuliana.

I am losing weight. I've lost more than a kilo over the past couple of months and I don't know why. What does it mean? Do you believe our minds can affect our bodies? Can a troubled heart make us sick? I am sick unto bloody death.

Stephen rubbed his mouth. George should look to himself before he criticized others. He was the one paralysed by cynicism and suspicion.

Do you remember the Masaccio fresco in the Brancacci Chapel? The one of Adam expelled from Paradise? Of course you must! I think of it now and it pains me more than I can say. I can see that face before me, weeping, buried in his hands and weeping. Surely, sorrow stems from ignorance of ourselves. Did Adam do wrong to want Knowledge?

I know things today that I didn't know then. I should have stayed with you. You were good for me. I could have fought off that man. I should not have let Sarah take over my life. It was as if I didn't have any say in the matter. And now she's off again, ruining someone else, as well as me.

You could say that it's knowing all this that makes me unhappy. But if I had been less ignorant to begin with then I would not be going through this now. I do not know what to do. I suppose I do not know myself.

He would see Giuliana soon, at that preview he'd agreed to attend. How long had it been since they'd last met? He tried to calculate, his mind disinclined for sums.

I can picture you in Rome. I read "Roman Fever" to you, do you remember? It helped me explain why I'd chosen the magnificent Edith for my thesis. Did you understand? A revelation of betrayal ... Yes, I have been betrayed, just as you predicted – but did you? I really can't remember anymore.

Andrew predicted it.

How angry you made me at my wedding! You only tried to warn, yet all I could do was pretend you didn't know me. How foolish I was – am. Am. AM! I don't know what I shall do. I don't know what I can do. It's as if I made the wrong decision a long time ago and now there's no going back. I have to follow where it leads, to the end of the line.

Don't I?

He looked at what he'd written, sneered at the words, his face full of contempt. *Delete. Are you sure?* He laughed. 'Yes, I'm bloody well sure.' A letter never sent. When he went to take another drink, he found he'd finished the last of the beer.

Number unobtainable.

He got ready for bed, but that bed – his, theirs – was no place for him. He'd be better off on the sofa. Laden with pillows and struggling with the quilt, he went downstairs to the sitting room, lay down and waited for sleep to come. He did not understand, could not grasp, the pain in his heart.

Half-awake, drunk on beer, he dreams he is a child, alone in bed upstairs, suddenly alert and wondering what is happening downstairs without him.

He walks to his father's room, hears the piano's mournful cries.

His father is at the keyboard, as he has been every day for weeks, seemingly no further advanced than when he began. His fingers stroke the keys, the hammers strike the wires, the chords echo and repeat, the silence shifts to accommodate the sounds, the hesitancies, the anger. Stephen can sense his father's frustration, his puzzlement with this inexplicable impotency, his fear that it will always be with him. It is like walking through a maze where every turning is a dead end, every meander a return to emptiness and useless discarded ideas. His father is locked inside and there is no way out, none. Finally, a slamming angry thrash at the piano, which howls his rage and pain and sorrow, then the crash of the lid, the bitter stepping away from the instrument of his own torture.

Stephen pushes the door wide and looks at him. His father turns, his thoughts somewhere with Audrey. Stephen knows this because that look comes into his father's face when he thinks of his mother, the look that says he can't find his way out of his jealous love, which makes Stephen blush with something other than confusion, he knows not what. His father is lonely and afraid. Stephen knows those feelings and can recognize them in others.

'Where's your sister?'

'In bed.'

His father nods, looks out the window at the twilit garden, the deep dark woods. 'In a minute, I'll go see how she is.' Suddenly, his face a mask.

When Stephen awoke, his mouth thick with uncleaned teeth and a stale tongue, his watch said 9 a.m. and Emma was standing in the doorway, looking at him, her face rigid with inexpression. He tried to smile, but facial movements, he discovered, made his head hurt. He felt at his hair, tapped at his bruise.

'What are you doing sleeping down here?' Her voice expressed suspicion, fear.

'I don't really know. I got home late, had a few beers ...'

'Where's Mum?'

'She was called away. A friend in trouble.'

'When will she be back?'

'Today, I should think. I've been trying to phone her.'

Emma looked at him, unblinking.

'No need to worry,' he told her. 'It's that same friend. Francesca – you know, the one with the exotic emotional life. She's probably stubbed her conscience and needs someone to rub it better.'

Lies. We're accomplished liars, Sarah and I. We have that much in common.

Emma continued to look blank. He tried to smile again. 'Please can you look at my head? I hit it last night and I can't see the damage.' He sat up, held his head down while Emma walked over. He felt her fingers part his hair, heard her breathing, smelled her perfume. Her black boots were scuffed at the toes.

'It's a big bruise.'

'Any blood?'

'No.'

'Thank God for that! And thank you, dear. Well ... if you'll excuse me, I'll try to rejoin the human race.'

'Stephen?'

'Yes?'

'Is everything all right?'

'All right?'

'With you and Mum?'

He looked at her sad and anxious face, smiled, wondered what to say. 'If I were to tell you everything is fine, would you believe me?'

Emma shook her head.

'Well, then, I won't. How were things with your father?'

'I had to get away. That's why I'm back. I'm going to go out with friends. I'll stay over with the Fromsetts.'

'Sounds good. Enjoy yourself. Phone me if you need anything, won't you?'

She nodded, ran upstairs, closed her door.

'Poor Emma! You have no abiding city.'

An hour later, he was sitting on Lorna's sofa, across from Paul's favourite chair. There was an insistent whine of cooking equipment from behind the door to the kitchen. It mingled with the turmoil in his stomach, which had started to ache as soon as the morning cold had forced its way inside him. He kept his eyes on his hands, held flat in his lap, while he contemplated what to say and how to say it. His arms were trembling, and it was hard to think. He looked at his phone again, flicked to Sarah's number, watched her name, switched off.

He stood up, went to the window. The world outside was about its business. A sudden wave of anger swept over him. It surged and swelled, then settled deep down inside him. The noise from the kitchen pierced his brain and set him wondering. He walked through to Lorna. 'What the hell ...'

Lorna was standing at the table, an electric whisk turning in her hand, whisking the air above an empty glass bowl. The oven was on full blast, empty, its door gaping. The microwave span with nothing in it. A food mixer and a blender were burning out their motors by the hob, all its rings illuminated. The toaster popped up, with no toast. The noise was awful, everywhere.

Lorna shouted at him: 'Everything's got to burn! It's the only way!'

'Lorna, for God's sake! What are you doing?' Stephen rushed round the table, switched off the oven, unplugged the toaster. Lorna watched him, frowning and open mouthed. When everything had fallen silent he reached for the whisk she held like a six-shooter. He prised it out of her clenched fingers and put it aside.

She looked angry, then her face crumpled and she was wailing. 'Oh, Stephen, Stephen! What can I do?'

He put his arm around her waist, rested his hand on her shoulder. 'Come and sit down. I'll make us some coffee.'

While he waited for the kettle to boil he wondered if Lorna really needed to know what he'd come to tell her. She was sitting at the end of the sofa and watched him put the tray down on the table at her side. He handed her a cup and sat down next to her.

Stephen drank his coffee and watched her eyes. They looked

troubled, as if she saw things beyond the room and without remedy. And now here he was to add to the load she was already unable to carry.

She began to look around the room in that way she had and for which she had been teased, mercilessly, by Paul and Sarah, by him. 'Relax, Lorna,' they'd tell her. 'Everything's perfect.' She would laugh, shamefaced, but a minute later she'd be at it again, wondering if something wasn't quite in the right place, whether the table needed polishing, if the carpet needed a clean. An unplumped cushion was sufficient to plunge her into existential angst, until she could resist no more and got up to fix it.

'The sitting room is immaculate as usual,' Stephen told her now, smiling, but this time she didn't seem to hear. She stood up, paced around the room, sat down on the edge of her seat. She lifted the pot of coffee from the tray and poured them both a second cup. 'It's decaf,' she told him, in a flat voice.

Paul's intangible presence made itself felt. Stephen could see him in that empty chair, his ironic smile directed at Lorna, his long legs crossed. He had the knack of being with the rest of them but remaining detached, talking only when he could insert a joke or a putdown, tell a humorous anecdote at his own expense. Paul had been a watcher.

Lorna's voice startled him. 'Thanks for coming over. I'm sorry about ... what happened earlier.'

Stephen swallowed some coffee and felt it drop to his stomach. The pain was hot and sharp, unmoving. 'That's all right. I wanted to speak to you anyway ...'

'What's wrong with Sarah's friend?'

Stephen shrugged. 'Sarah didn't say. I've been trying to contact them both, but no luck. She has – I don't know what you'd call them, really – emotional crises? They both take them seriously. Perhaps they're right. I'm no help, apparently, so Sarah doesn't tell me much anymore.'

This was wrong. He was conniving with a lie. 'Where's Paul?'

'Away on business. Back in two days.'

The urge to tell Lorna was overwhelming, as if he had no choice but to scream at her, 'Sarah! It's Sarah! Are you satisfied?'

Lorna was crying silent tears. She glanced at him while she pulled a tissue from her apron pocket. 'I'm sorry. Excuse me.'

Stephen put down his cup, his stomach stabbing at him while he leaned over the table. He drew closer to Lorna. 'Tell me what's the matter, won't you? I'd like to help if I can.'

Lorna opened her mouth, put her clenched fist to her lips, the tissue showing white between her fingers. A moment later she took hold of herself, sat straight, cleared her throat. 'It's Paul. He's seeing someone else.'

'Oh?'

Lorna looked at him. 'You don't sound surprised! Has he said anything to you?'

'No. I haven't – I haven't really talked to him since our anniversary. What makes you think –?'

'Business trips are not this frequent. I checked with his office. Caught him out in ... lies.' Lorna waved her hand in a vague manner. 'There are other things ... No need to say what they are. I've noticed them. Thought nothing of them. Didn't want to know. Didn't want to think about them, make the connections. But now ... I can't ignore them anymore. There are too many and I don't know what to do.'

Stephen, breathless, placed his hand over Lorna's. 'Do you know who it is?'

Lorna shook her head. 'I don't want to know. As long as I can't picture her ... picture them, together ... then it's not quite real. I can pretend it's not ... betrayal – or worse.'

'Yes. I see what you mean. Even so, if you knew –'

Lorna laughed a bitter laugh. 'Do you want to know something funny? I once thought it might be Sarah. They've always got on, haven't they?'

'It is Sarah, Lorna,' he whispered, appalled at himself, his face blushing.

Had she heard him? He searched Lorna's face for signs of comprehension. She looked at him strangely, as if unable to take in the words. She smiled, shook her head at him. Her mouth opened. 'Surely you've seen the way he looks at her? Unlike me, Sarah is an attractive woman.'

'What? Did you hear ...?' Her eyes looked wild and empty. They confused him. 'You're the best of us all ... You're a lovely person. A good heart is the sun and the moon. And that's Shakespeare, so you can believe it.'

'But good looks don't need the sun and the moon, do they?'

Stephen shrugged. 'Give me a good heart any day.'

'Men say that, but they don't mean it. Look at Paul. Look at you.'

Stephen frowned. 'Me? What do you mean?'

Lorna licked her lips, her eyes sharp with reflected light. 'Well ... what I mean is – you must have noticed – Sarah does have quite a ruthless streak to her – wouldn't you say?'

Stephen swallowed, glanced at the empty chair. 'Where is he now?'

'Who knows!'

'Have you phoned him?'

'Of course I've phoned him! I've phoned him until I'm blue in the face. I can't get through. Are you sure he hasn't said anything to you?'

'No, he's said nothing.'

'I keep going over and over in my mind what it is I could have done wrong.'

'It's not you who's done wrong, surely?'

'Is he just tired of me? After twelve years? I thought we were happy. We were happy, I *know* we were! He's not said anything to you?'

'No.'

'This has been going on months. Lots of months. At least.'

'That's what I thought.'

Lorna looked at him, frowned her confusion, shook her head again. 'I suppose I should just wait until it's over – if it ever is over. The thought of doing something – talking about it – makes me curl up inside.' She dabbed at her eyes, suddenly angry with herself, it seemed to Stephen, for doing so. 'The stupid sorry bastard! What does he think he's playing at? It's so pathetic. At his age!'

Stephen cleared his throat. 'I'm going to talk to him. As soon as I can.'

'No! I don't want you to get mixed up in our problems.'

'I'm already mixed up in them. We all are.'

Lorna gazed at the coffee things. 'What would you say?'

Stephen put his arm on the back of the sofa. 'All sorts of things. And a punch on the nose wouldn't go amiss, either.'

'He'd probably give you one back.'

He could feel himself boiling inside, as if Lorna had given him her anger and confusion.

They sat in silence.

A minute later, Lorna's mouth opened and she swayed forward, her eyes newly weeping. Stephen caught hold of her before she fell, held his arms about her shoulders, and found himself crying with her, great silent tears dropping to his shirtfront.

'There is no good way out of this,' Stephen told them. 'It's the same for me, believe me. But it will come to an end. For both of us. Whatever happens, a contented life – what I mean is, it will end.'

Lorna curled herself into his arms. He could feel her breath on his neck, while her hair tickled his face. She clutched at him and he patted her back mechanically, all the time afraid she had heard what he'd told her, disappointed that she hadn't. He was angry for her, for them both. Then she lifted her mouth to his and began to kiss him in short breathy bursts of passion. Gently, he placed his hand to the back of her head and steered her away from his face. Hot tears fell on his neck.

Eventually calmed, Lorna pulled away and stood up. 'A contented life? That's what I thought I had. Seems I was wrong. But you're a good man, Stephen. Thank you.'

Outside, in a cold wind, he tried again. Number unobtainable.

10

Stephen stood in his mother's attic by the single window at the gable end. It was cold up here; he could see his breath rising through the torn cobwebs trailing in the rafters. He'd borrowed his father's gardening coat, still kept in the hall. It was too large for him and the stale aroma of pipe tobacco clung to the collar. The pockets felt dry, with traces of earth where his fingernails dug into the seams.

Ella and Billie had followed him up the stairs, clattered around the wooden floor, sniffing at everything, enjoying the fuss. Then the aroma of cooking had sent them shooting down to the kitchen.

'Traitors!'

He'd turned on the light – a single unshaded bulb that stained the late afternoon gloom a grubby nicotine yellow. Walking around, his feet rasping on the grit-strewn boards, he looked about him. An old rocking horse stood to one side, mane all pulled out, the paint faded and scratched. The dull glass eyes looked alarmed when he rocked it back and forth, its springs whining, the rockers thudding. An assortment of old furniture he couldn't remember was piled in the far corner, thick with dust and powdery mould. Only the solid oak wardrobe looked familiar; through the gaping doors he saw a jumble of wire hangers on the rusting rail.

He looked up. He did not trust that roof, kept examining it for signs of betrayal, incipient collapse. It was bowing over the main beam, the spaces between tiles bulging with daylight. That old beam had warped, apparently harmlessly, a local builder had pronounced one morning, when his mother had grown worried by the thought of rain beating into her bedroom. It would last for generations yet, she'd been told, smilingly, with the gentle condescension of a practical man who knew his business. Still, it didn't look right and neither she nor Stephen – ashamed of the ignorance that nourished his doubts – quite believed it would survive another year.

Exterior sounds entered insidiously up here, at the top of a house beneath an ancient roof. A train revving in the station, the cry of a wheeling bird, the sough of traffic on the distant main road, felt intimate and menacing. The world outside searched him out, pressed patiently at stone and wood, seeped in beneath the eaves and surged through the attic. The sounds of its coming were like his invisible throng of troubles flying home to roost.

Stephen, on edge, listened, his body shivering beneath his father's coat. He saw a cloud of dust kicked up by a draught from the staircase. He could have closed the door, but the thought of being shut in tight like that disturbed him. He preferred to see the banisters outlined against the diffuse light palely loitering by the gothic window on the landing.

He checked his phone, thought of Lorna, desperate in her empty neat house. He dialled her number. She assured him she was all right.

'Sarah dropped by,' she told him.

'She did? But I've been trying to call her all day.'

'Her friend's not feeling that bad, apparently.'

'Did you tell her – what you told me?'

'Yes. You've both been so good. She was terribly shocked. And very sympathetic.'

'I bet she was!' Stephen leant against the wardrobe and paused for breath. 'I left her a note. I'm at my mother's. I'll be back tomorrow evening. Did she know?'

'Yes, she knows.'

'Well, I'll try to phone her again.'

'Stephen? I had a dream ... I mean, did you say ...? Did I imagine? I thought you told me – it was her.'

Stephen's heart beat out his frustration. What was wrong with this woman? 'It was no dream, dear. I did say that.'

'Oh!'

There was a long silence. He thought of her in tears, and all those kitchen implements waiting for her annihilating anger.

'Lorna, please don't do anything until I get back. Promise.'

'What could I do?'

'Promise?'

'All right. But when ...?'

'I'll come home today and speak to Sarah.'

Stephen hung up. He heard a creak on the staircase, listened intently, heard nothing more. 'Mother? Are you there?'

He began to phone home, stopped himself, shoved the phone into his dirty pocket. He'd had enough. After so many attempts to speak to Sarah, now that it looked like he could, he could no longer remember what he wanted to say. Instead, he felt another surge of fury. He wanted to shout, but Audrey might hear, so he whispered all the foul names he would call his wife, until he was exhausted. George had been right. The time for thinking was long since past and he had to act – and in the heat. He would return home early and confront the rotten truth.

He sighed, looked at the floor at his feet. This corner was full of Audrey's show business memorabilia. He hadn't seen any of it in years, and gazing at it now he realized there was more here than he'd ever seen. It spilled out of suitcases with broken locks, hung bent and begrimed from battered cardboard boxes ripped at the corners – photographs, press cuttings, posters, record covers – the ephemeral detritus of a life stopped in its tracks. He watched it all dimming in the fading light of evening with a kind of hopeless amazement. It was like watching someone else's dream disintegrate, turning to dust and mould.

He bent down and took hold of a handful of paper. None of this stuff had interested him when Audrey was still singing – still less when she was in the worst of her depression. Now, curiously, he had taken a fancy to it, and he'd formed a vague desire to sort through everything. It provided a kind of comfort. He couldn't put it any more definitely than that, although he'd had an excuse at the ready.

'I want to find some publicity photos of you to show Emma,' he'd told his mother.

'Help yourself, if you can find them.'

All such things had been despatched to the attic once Audrey's illness and drinking had taken over her family's lives, when visible reminders of what once had been were enough to send her into another binge, another fury, another misery. Within a few minutes of sifting through it all he'd found were a few photographs of Audrey in her prime, when her hair had been thick and lustrous, her skin perfect, her eyes unrheumed. She smiled in these pictures, and her smile gave no hint of what lay ahead, so close as hardly to be the future at all. Stephen looked at this glamorous woman, his own young mother. She was Audrey – she must be – but it was hard to tell. Time and some fatal mistakes committed by someone somewhere had done their work. He sighed, wondered if the past is always sad to contemplate, or whether that was just him, from the vantage point of his own hopelessness. Audrey looked past him with bright uncomprehending faith, destiny's child. At least she had achieved something in her life, however brief. If a woman had that to look back on then she had the right to feel proud.

Borne on wings of alcohol, his mother's voice clawed up at him from the foot of the stairs. 'Stephen! What on earth are you doing up there? Come down!'

'In a minute!'

Audrey had not asked why he had appeared suddenly at her door, without warning. He had been prepared for the usual interrogation and questioning looks, but she had held her tongue and he had been grateful. His mother had kept a tight rein on her suspicions, which had surely cost her quite an effort. She'd welcomed him with a glass of wine – a bottle already open on the kitchen table – and the promise of a big hot meal, 'cooked with my own fair hands.' She'd held them up for him to see, then grimaced when she saw the thick fingers, the grave marks clustered in the crackled skin. She'd slurped at her wine and told him he was too skinny to be alive.

'I'm no thinner now than when I was a teenager.'

'That was decades ago! I'll add to the veg. And there's some ice cream in the freezer. We need to feed you up, boy.'

Stephen put aside three of the best shots of his mother, including a photograph of Audrey with her usual quintet: vibes, trombone, piano, drums and double bass. It was a studio shot, obviously posed. The band was only pretending to play, while his mother was frozen in a carefully planned gesture of spontaneity, arms raised, head to one side. He looked at their faces and recognized just one of them.

Ronnie Butterman was on bow fiddle in those days, part of the regular set of musicians who backed Audrey. Stephen looked at his generous face with its thick lips and sleepy grey eyes. He remembered how he'd met Zinc, as he was known, once or twice, never for long. All he could recall was that big smile and a booming laugh. Zinc had half-shares in a couple of Parisian jazz bars, and he planned to retire there and play the bass on his own stage. Stephen's father had told him that one summer evening, when both of them were dreaming at the piano, left alone while Audrey was away performing. His dad liked Zinc, liked all musicians, no matter what they were like personally, as long as they could play and lose themselves in the music. With the house so far out in the sticks, it was rare to see any of them at home, but there had been times when they'd stayed over and their music had floated up to Stephen's bedroom, where he lay awake. Now he thought about it, he could see Zinc arriving in a thick long coat and carrying his bass like a curvaceous coffin. Stephen had dared to lift it inside the house and almost fallen with the weight. He remembered Zinc laughing and, the next morning, seeing him at the breakfast table, all alone, wearing a red dressing gown and a thoughtful expression.

Stephen shuddered. It was dark outside and the cold was worse. He put out the light, closed the door and went down to the kitchen, where Audrey was in full swing at the hob and the wine. The air was thick with vapour and the insistent aroma of leek and onion tart.

'Mother, what became of Ronnie Butterman?'

Stephen sat at the table and watched as Audrey stirred something red and viscous in a shallow frying pan. He had offered his services as sous chef, but Audrey refused help, as she had developed a passion for cooking, which Stephen encouraged. As long as she was cooking, her drinking could be confined to slurps of wine. He thanked Mrs McDougall for Audrey's new-found interest, as it was she who had helped Audrey and lavished praise on her pastry.

Audrey gazed thoughtfully at the cooker hood, her eyes narrowed. 'Zinc? He died ... ten years back. Cancer. When I think of all that smoke we used to breathe in when we were performing, I wonder how any of us survived. I must have smoked a couple of hundred a day.'

'Did he ever get to Paris?'

'Yes. He lived his dream for a while.' Audrey turned off the heat and stood staring into space, wooden spoon in hand. 'God! He was a great guy. Best bassist I ever had. With him behind us, it was like no one could do any wrong. Those big ugly fingers of his were magic.' She smiled, then snapped back from her reverie, looked at him, eyes sharp. 'Why?'

'Oh, nothing. I have his photograph here.'

Audrey looked at him for a long moment, then shuffled to the table, refilled her glass, added to Stephen's, still half-full from when he'd left it. She looked through the pictures, smiling. 'For Emma? Tell her she can keep them. Oh! There he is!' She admired Zinc and the rest of the band. 'The places I travelled with those guys! All over Europe. And the things we did! Life on the road in those days was a lot of laughs.'

Audrey pointed with a pastried finger. 'Ronnie. Charlie Pierce on drums. Ray Nicholls on vibes. Paris Mitchell on slide trombone. Geoff Keogh on piano. That must have been after your dad decided to call it a day.' Audrey sighed. 'They don't make 'em like that anymore.'

Ella and Billie clipped in together, looked around, lay themselves on their blankets beneath the radiator.

'You know,' said Stephen, 'there's a lot of this stuff upstairs. Someone should sort through it.'

Audrey swallowed another mouthful of wine. 'Not me.'

'I could, one day. I'm good at raking over other people's pasts. Like with Edith Wharton.'

'You rake over your own past. Leave mine alone.'

'You're the one who's always going on about it. I wish you wouldn't.'

'The old girl has to live in the present, is that it? What's so good about now, I'd like to know? You'll understand when you get to be my age.'

'Can anyone get to be your age?'

They both laughed. Stephen checked his messages. Nothing.

'Ever since you arrived you've been playing with that bloody phone. Can't you leave it alone? You get more like Emma every day.'

'Sorry.'

Audrey looked at him, unmoving, her glass held to her cheek, her face expressionless. Then she patted his shoulder, clumsily, returned to the stove, kept busy, talking and drinking.

'Old age is a terrible thing, Stephen. Don't go there.'

'You make it sound like a crime.'

'That's exactly what it is.'

'At least you've had the privilege to get old. Many poor souls never make it.'

'I'd rather burn out than fade away.'

'It's possible to burn out *and* fade away. Did you think of that?'

Audrey laughed, took another drink. 'No, I never did. In my business – I don't just mean jazz, I mean show business – you see all sorts of things. People kill themselves in all sorts of ways. Some do it quick ...'

'Quickly ...'

'... and others slow.'

'There are worse things than murder. A man can be killed a little at a time, inch by inch.'

Stephen glanced up and caught Audrey looking at him. She turned away. 'How's your job? Have you got that promotion yet?'

'I'm working on it. I don't know if I want it.'

'Why not?'

'For one thing, it's too much hard work. Boring hard work. I don't want to gain a pro vice-chancellorship and lose my soul.'

Stephen resisted the urge to check his phone. Instead, he made himself think about the job. He couldn't make up his mind. He couldn't make up his mind about anything these days. 'It's like I've reached a fork in the road and don't know where each one leads and which one to take.' As soon as he heard the words he wondered if they were true.

Audrey had stopped listening and moved on. 'Life is always on the raw side when you're a performer,' she told him over her shoulder. 'There are too many feelings flying around begging to be felt. You get tired. You fend off nervous exhaustion as best you can. Drugs. Booze. Love. That's it, I guess.'

'That's all over with now, Mother.'

Audrey shrugged, grimaced at her empty glass. 'Habits outlast their usefulness. They don't let you go, no matter how hard you try. Then you stop trying.'

'I wish you'd tried a little harder, for all our sakes.'

Audrey cackled. 'But then I wouldn't have been me.'

She was pretty far gone by the time she served the meal. They ate in the kitchen. It was the warmest room in the house and the glow of the pelmet lighting beneath the cupboards was soft and friendly. Audrey found another bottle of red and gave it to Stephen to open. 'I'll try harder tomorrow.'

Stephen poured the wine.

Audrey drank, ate. 'How's Emma?' She waited while Stephen munched through a mouthful of vegetables.

'Fine. More or less. As far as I can tell.'

'I do worry about her. There's so much pressure on young people these days.'

'Things aren't going well between her and her parents. She's spending the weekend with friends, but ... I don't know. It seems to me she's too isolated.'

'She's got you.'

'She can't – doesn't – depend on me all the time. She needs

people her own age.'

'She could bring someone with her at Christmas.'

'I already told her that. I don't know if she wants to.'

Audrey poured herself another glass. 'You should have had children of your own.'

Stephen shrugged. 'It takes two, Mother.'

Audrey nodded, staring at nothing. 'Sarah never felt comfortable as a mother. I can tell.' Her voice grew innocent: 'How is she?'

'Okay. Busy. This is wonderful food by the way.'

'She'll be coming for Christmas, right?'

'I don't know.'

'Stephen! Make her!'

'I can't force her to come if she doesn't want to.'

'But why doesn't she want to? You'll be here and Emma ...'

'And you.'

'Don't blame me for the state of your marriage.'

Stephen looked up from his plate.

'Oh yes! I can tell. You're looking at an expert. I've seen more relationships crack up than you'll ever know. People get that same look – the one you've got now.'

'Don't dramatize, Mother.'

'I'm right, aren't I?'

'I don't want to talk about it.'

'Well I do want to talk about it. What's going on?'

'We're just having problems, that's all.'

'You never should have married her. If I could have I would have prevented you. Sarah's too singleminded, everything's in her head. She's too cold, too calculating, too ...'

'Too much like you.'

'If I believed that I'd really take to drink. What's the matter, one of you fooling around?'

'Mother!'

'It's her, isn't it? That's why you're here. She's off somewhere and you've come home. Hah!'

Stephen, his heart racing, tried to remain impassive. Every now and then, usually when she'd been drinking, Audrey came out with something so preposterously accurate, so painfully to the point, it was as if she'd been reading his thoughts. Perhaps that was why Sarah didn't like her. Maybe it had happened to her, too.

'You'll be on your best behaviour at Christmas, won't you, Mother?'

Audrey looked at him darkly.

'What I mean is, try not to say out loud everything you're thinking. Especially to Angela and Buzz.'

'I'll say what the hell I like, when I like, in my own house.'

'Please, Mother. Let's all try to be nice.'

'Nice? Where does nice get you?'

Afterwards, Stephen washed the dishes. He could hear Audrey in the sitting room, warbling a song he didn't know, and the clink of bottles in the drinks cabinet. He found her slumped in the sofa, a glass of whiskey in her hand and a half-empty bottle at her feet. She looked sleepy, her eyes dark slits where the makeup had congealed. She was mumbling. He sat at the other end of the sofa and stared at her half-closed eyes. 'How did it come to this, Mother? You there and me here. We make a fine pair, you and I. Perhaps we serve each other right.'

Audrey hiccoughed, gestured vaguely with her free hand. 'Those guys ... we must have travelled thousands of miles. Europe ... all those jazz festivals. They loved us ... Jim? Jim grew tired ... tired with everything. Not his fault. Either you like the life or you don't. Even so ... a dirty shame ... those hands of Zinc's! He slapped that bow fiddle like no one else. Even Ed Thigpen said so. Zinc said, "Ed's a drummer. What does he know?" But he was pleased ...'

Stephen listened to his mother breathing. 'Fall asleep, Audrey, for God's sake.' He sat back, began to doze.

He hears someone in the hallway, heels on the quarry tiles. He looks through the open door and sees Giuliana coming towards him, Ella and Billie behind her, their ears pricked. She is in white, as he always remembers her, but her hair is different somehow and she looks older. Her face is lined with fear.

'Stephen! Help me! He'll be here soon. Get up!' She pulls at his arms, glances back over her shoulder. 'Stephen! Oh why don't you get up!'

Stephen's head jerked uncomfortably. He could hear someone speaking stifled words, as if their mouth were full of broken china.

'Stephen!'

He opened his eyes, looked around and wondered where he was.

His mother stirred, let slip her glass, spilling the last of her drink into her lap. 'God! Strong warm hands ... he couldn't keep them off me. It's okay ... these things happen. Too many feelings ... I couldn't do anything about the baby, Jim! Zinc wouldn't let me. He would have left the band, he said. But I didn't want ... everything so messed up. Poor Jim.'

Another secret out. Stephen looked at Audrey and tried to picture her in Zinc's arms. All he could remember was his father's inscrutable face and the sound of a crashing piano lid. Then Zinc himself, in a red dressing gown, looking thoughtful. He wondered if he should tell his sister – half-sister. Ignorance, he knew, was a kind of refuge.

He sighed, took his mother's glass, picked up the bottle and put them in the kitchen. When he returned, she had slumped over, face in a cushion, snoring. He shook her, then placed her arm around his shoulders, half-walking, half-carrying her to her bedroom. She felt heavy, and he thought of his own thin body buckling under the weight of Audrey one day, until his mother crushed him. He put her on the bed, took off her shoes and left her in her clothes. There was some makeup remover on the dressing table. He swabbed it over her face, until the awful raddled truth emerged from behind its painted mask.

He checked his watch. There were still a few minutes left before the late train home.

11

Stephen closed his eyes and waited for sleep. Each time the train slowed he was pushed forward in his seat, and all at once he would awaken, confused by the noise and the close airless warmth, the smell of lifeless plastic and cold hard metal. Dazed, he would stare across a deserted car park or a straggling belt of trees, while the engine panted beneath a yellow wash of sodium vapour light. A minute later, heaving itself with a great bellow and convulsion, his train would lumber onwards into the night. The journey home was a long dark tunnel, striped with lonely painted stations.

Somewhere down the line he was dragged from oblivion once too often, and he woke up for good. His mind would not keep on track. His thoughts meandered like the invisible river that wound through the valley beside the railway, crossing beneath it, wandering into forest dark and silent, then snaking back in tight coils of stoney winter water. He followed them where they led, stirred to anger, sadness, humiliation by a flood of associations.

Audrey's face appeared to him as she lay asleep on her bed, the quilt sprinkled with yesterday's drinks and a week's worth of dog hairs. He hoped she would be all right. It had been hard to leave her, dishevelled and bedevilled, but then she always made him feel guilty, deep down inside himself, where he couldn't reach. Audrey would have accused him of neglect, would no doubt do so the next time they spoke, forgetting the years when she'd doled out abandonment for everyone except herself.

His mother's inspired guesswork about his marriage had unnerved him. His troubles always turned to acid in his stomach when she held them up before him, clothed in words flippant and dismissive, as if his life and unhappiness were his own affair, and certainly his own stupid fault.

Stephen sighed. Audrey never suspected how cruel she could be.

From Audrey to Sarah. He tried to trace his lawfully wedded troubles back to their source, asked when everything began to go wrong, but could there really be a single point of origin for something so momentously awful? As he remembered his life with Sarah, their past rows reared up at him in all their old fury; harsh words now spoke bitterly as if they had just that minute been spat at him. Ten years' worth of grudges, the vast span of injustice and resentment, felt new and raw. Even things he thought he'd forgiven and forgotten burst into flame and clamoured for his outrage – the times Sarah had made fun of his family in front of their friends, or when she'd walked out of a restaurant halfway through their anniversary meal, spilling her wine into his lap. He began to brood, and soon he found himself putting thoughts into Sarah's mind, words into her mouth, inventing further confrontations, finding new reasons to be angry with her. As if he didn't already have enough of those.

'For God's sake, stop!' His head burned behind his eyes.

There wasn't much comfort anywhere, as far as he could see. His family, Christmas, the job – it all felt hollow, a waste of effort that would lead him nowhere. When he put a hand to his stomach he could feel the turmoil surging through him. He stood up, stretched, walked the length of the empty swaying carriage and stood at one of the doors as the first lights of the city swung through the dark.

'Aaargh!'

Stephen was, he felt, at the end of his rope.

He walked from the railway station through a persistent cold wind that made his eyes water. Frost lay thick on parked cars, glittered in blocked gutters, glinted on pavements. Winter had pounced and ice was clutching at his heart.

Sarah had been clever. She had sought to allay Lorna's suspicions and arranged to make her own innocence appear beyond doubt – returning home alone, playing the confidante, while Paul remained away for another day. Such tactics required immense reserves of guile. It suddenly felt as if he didn't know and had never known this person. Had he imagined her, that blameless woman he'd loved?

As he came nearer to home his nervousness got the better of him. What would he find? What, really, did he hope to find? Catching the two of them in the act had sounded fine when he'd imagined himself as righteously angry, filled with steely determination. But now, when he was cold and tired and more than a little drunk, it all seemed changed, and he didn't feel ready for anything apart from warmth and sleep.

He stood outside his unlit home and looked through the uncurtained windows. Its dark rooms were full of angular grey shadows. A mirror caught the light of a streetlamp and threw it back tired and tarnished. There were no suspicious cars in the drive; the patch of front garden with its stone lion on guard outside the porch looked calm and innocent. He held his breath, watched and waited. Nothing moved. He expelled his breath and walked to the door.

When he let himself in he could tell immediately the house was empty. While he prowled through his home and found it as he'd left it, he wondered why he'd never noticed before how squalid it was. This had not been the way he wanted to live – clutter and ugliness lay strewn about him, glared at him from the walls and ceilings. He was a stranger in his own home.

He made up another bed on the sofa, setting the alarm for six o'clock. Lying there in the dark, his neck at an awkward angle against the corner cushion, he wondered what the morning would bring. He felt alone, profoundly lost and with no help from anyone. His eyes watered, while his thoughts about his life and marriage continued where'd they'd left off until he fell asleep.

Late the next morning the phone rang.

'Hello Stephen, it's George. Have you heard?'

Stephen suppressed a yawn. If George was phoning about his job prospects he'd tell him to get lost. 'Morning George. Heard what?'

'A student's killed himself. Found hanging in his parents' garage.'

Stephen sat down on the arm of a chair. 'Who is it?'

'Jack Caswell ... Hello? Are you there?'

Stephen gazed through the window to the winter weather. It was cold and wet, with a fine misty rain that drifted on the wind. 'Yes, I'm here.' He cleared his throat, ran a hot hand across his brow. 'When did it happen?'

'Sometime last night. His parents found him.'

Stephen heard George telling him what little he knew. Jack had perhaps sunk to ultimate despair while he, Stephen, was safely dozing in a railway carriage. The possibility made the news even worse, somehow. He thought then of Emma, how precious she was and how alone in the world. Nothing must be allowed to hurt her. 'Will there be an inquest?'

'I expect so.'

Stephen suddenly felt intensely angry at the news. Jack had got out – that was fine for him. What about the people he'd left behind? It was such a stupid waste. Everything could have been sorted out – *was* being sorted out. He should have believed what Stephen had told him, should have hung on to that moment of glory when he spoke for the first time in class and astonished them all.

Stephen stood up and kicked the chair. Then he saw Paul's car pull up before the house. 'George, I have to go. We'll speak about this tomorrow.'

'What's up? Has something happened?'

'It's just about to. Tell you tomorrow.'

Stephen hung up and stood back from the window. He could, he thought, hear the purr of the engine, and then when it was cut, a silence beneath the swish of the wind and drizzle. Two young mothers walked by pushing buggies, all hoods and laughter and rain-soaked jeans. The car's windows began to fog.

For a long time no one emerged. Then the passenger door opened and Sarah appeared, carrying the bag she took whenever she stayed away for a day or two. He looked at her and saw his lovely wife – yes, despite everything, she was lovely and she knew it. Her hair was a mess and looked as if it had already been caught in the rain, but she was Sarah, the same as yesterday and tomorrow. She stood on the pavement waiting, barely glancing at the house, until Paul got out and they walked to the door. Stephen watched them coming towards him. He had never seen them alone before, he suddenly recalled, and they were contented with one another and pleased with their own thoughts, as he could remember being, a long time ago. Sarah was talking and Paul was nodding and smiling. Their happiness shocked him.

Breathing heavily, he hid behind the study door. He started to tremble, while his heart raced and made his chest ache. His sagging belt buckle clattered against the door, until he clutched it to his stomach. He heard the front door open and the muffled sound of voices. The door closed, bags were dropped to the floor, coats were removed. Then Sarah called 'Stephen!' and 'Emma?' It all sounded so natural that Stephen wondered for an instant if he'd been imagining things, that perhaps incredibly there was an innocent explanation for everything. Then his anger rushed back at him.

Sarah spoke quietly. 'Stay here. I'll just check.'

He heard her climb the stairs and walk about. 'They're not here!' she called down from the landing, evidently relieved. 'Let's have some coffee.'

Paul was ironic and smug. 'Do you think that's a good idea?'

'Don't worry,' Sarah replied breathlessly as she hurried downstairs. Noises in the kitchen.

Stephen, abruptly conscious of the ridiculousness of the situation, thought of Polonius behind the arras in *Hamlet*, and wondered what to do. He couldn't remain hidden indefinitely, but he had to pick his moment. Undecided, he fidgeted while he considered the possibilities, and knocked his toe against the bottom of the door. It sounded like the boom of a cannon. He held his breath and strained his ears, but no one reacted. A minute later he had slipped through to the hallway under cover of the noise from the kettle and stationed himself behind the half-closed door to the kitchen, from where he could see Paul sitting at the table, legs crossed, reading the front page of the newspaper that lay folded on his knee. He looked at home. Sarah was setting things up for coffee.

'When's he coming back exactly?' Paul asked, not looking up.

'This evening. I don't know the time.'

'What about her?'

'I don't know. Probably this afternoon, if she shows up at all.'

'I'd better get going after I've drunk this.'

'Do you have to?'

Stephen had heard enough. The little mew of regret in Sarah's question told him all he needed to know. He watched them a while longer, furious and fascinated by their air of inviolability. That they had no idea he was there, observing them, gave him strength. They sat at the table and shared the paper. Everything looked ordinary. It was if they were married already. Then he noticed they'd removed their shoes in the hall and their legs were interlaced, Sara's foot resting provocatively, negligently, in Paul's lap.

Stephen stepped out from behind the door, centre stage. 'He's back already!' he announced, arms spread wide, face beaming.

Sarah jumped in her chair. Her shocked expression froze for a moment, before she closed her gaping mouth and attempted a bright and brittle smile. She removed her foot from Paul's lap. 'Stephen! How nice! Would you like –'

Paul had turned round in his chair, glassy eyed and red in the face.

'Good morning, Friend!' Stephen told him. 'I talked to your dear wife. She's learned you're having an affair and wanted my advice. I told her I'd have a word with you and give you this.'

Stephen punched Paul on the nose, hard and fast, before he could think about it and tell himself no. Blood exploded over Paul's face as he cried out, fell back in his chair and tumbled to the floor. Stephen found himself kneeling beside him and punching Paul again in the face, the body. Overwhelming energy coursed through him. Paul squirmed and shouted, tried to protect his face. Stephen felt Sarah's hands on his arms, the heat of her coffee-tainted breath as she shouted in his ear: 'Stop it! Stop it!' He pushed her off and punched Paul again, who lay now with his head against the base of the fridge, his legs trapped beneath his upturned chair. Stephen wanted to inflict pain in a way he had never felt before. All the rage he had failed to find until this moment was there suddenly at the ends of his clenched fists. He pushed Sarah off again, noticed the steel coffee pot on the table to his side. It was heavy and still hot. He held it high and watched as Paul's blood pulsed from his broken nose, over his face, onto his shirt, the floor.

'My name is Stephen!' he shouted. 'My daughter's name is Emma!'

Sarah screamed: 'Stop it, Stephen, stop it!'

Stephen fought her off again, then looked down at all the blood he'd shed, the coffee pot like a mace in his upturned hand. He swung down the pot in a great arc of his mighty righteous arm and watched it crash into the floor next to Paul's head. It made a clanging sound that pleased Stephen, so he did it again. Paul's eyes looked agreeably frightened.

Stephen got to his feet. Paul was whimpering and breathing heavily. Sarah was on the other side of the table, looking down at Paul. She was crying, moaning, 'You've killed him! You've bloody killed him!'

Once he'd got his breath back, he spoke to Paul. 'Got your car keys?'

Paul was unable to reply. Stephen patted Paul's pockets,

found the keys. He pushed past Sarah and dropped a roll of paper towels into Paul's lap. 'I want you the fuck out of my house. Go bleed in your own home.'

Paul applied the towels to his face. 'Stephen, one day ...'

'Shut the fuck up!' Stephen yelled.

After he'd pushed Paul out the door, he phoned Lorna and told her what had happened.

'You haven't hurt him?' Lorna gasped.

'Of course I've bloody hurt him! But ... well ... it looks worse than it is. Don't worry. It's up to you now.' He put the phone down and knew she would forgive Paul.

His heart was still racing, his elation fighting with his doubts. He had done something, at long last. Was it the right thing? Yes, yes, a thousand times yes! Remorse was stupid. It didn't matter if it was right or wrong. It felt good. He had impressed himself, he had acted. Then he started to shake and he felt himself crying. He couldn't stop. It felt like something old and rotten was leaving him.

Sarah had rushed off. A long time later he could hear the bath water running. He wandered to the kitchen and began to clean up the mess. 'I never knew the wanker had so much blood in him.' The buckled coffee pot had a fleck of red on the handle. He washed it off.

Sarah finally came downstairs, washed and changed. Her eyes

were red. 'You're an absolute bastard, Stephen, and I hate you. Do you hear? I hate you!'

He began to think of something to eat. 'I'm not going to talk to you now. I'm tired and I'm hungry and I don't want to say anything I'll regret.'

'You'll bloody well have to talk about it, you bastard! You nearly killed him!'

'A bloody nose is not ...'

'Put that fucking bread down and talk to me!'

'Not now. Emma will be home soon.'

'Fuck Emma!'

They faced each other across the kitchen table. He tried to find the words that would hurt. 'Have you thought of Lorna? She won't give up just like that, you know. She loves him – God knows why.'

'Love! How would you know? You can't love anyone. You wouldn't know how.'

'That's your opinion. I'm not going to talk now.'

'We have to, the sooner the better.'

'You've been content with silence up till now. Now it suits you, you want to talk. I'm afraid you'll just have to wait.'

Sarah shouted. 'What will you do, hit me?'

Stephen shouted back. 'If I have to, yes!' He found some cheese in the fridge and began to cut sandwiches. 'If it can happen to me, it could happen to you,' he mumbled.

'What?'

Stephen sighed. 'Something Andrew said. The poor bastard. It wasn't his fault – or mine.'

'Does it never occur to you that you're to blame?'

Stephen laughed. 'Oh I see! It's all my fault is it? I've just imagined you and Paul, have I?'

'You deserve it! That's what you get when you let things happen instead of making them. It was always me ...You don't know how to feel – you never have.'

'I've been learning pretty quickly over the last few weeks.'

'You're so bloody oblivious, Stephen! Does anything matter to you? Apart from Edith Bloody Wharton?'

'Plenty of things matter to me. You mattered, for a start. Emma. My mother. My work.'

'And bloody Juliana Borderaux whatever her name is.'

'That's Henry James, not Edith Wharton.'

'Don't be so fucking pedantic!'

Stephen heard the front door close. A minute later Emma appeared. 'Hello dear! Did you have a good time?'

Emma nodded, glanced from one to the other of them and backed out of the kitchen. She ran up the stairs, slammed her bedroom door.

'Now see what you've done.'

Sarah looked down, her head in her hand. 'If you've hurt him …'

'It's safe to say he deserved it, the sneaking bastard. Besides, it's nothing serious. Don't dramatize.'

'All that blood!'

'That's why you hit the nose first. It disables your opponent.'

Sarah began to cry.

'Shouldn't you be thinking about your daughter? You'll have the time, now that you don't have to pretend you're writing that bloody useless book of yours.'

Stephen felt ravenously hungry. He bit into a sandwich. ' Do you know, I feel – I feel like I can put on weight now.'

Sarah looked at him in disgust.

And so they continued, long into the night. It would be the measure of their days until they came to a decision about their future.

He did not sleep.

The next morning he walked down the corridor to George's office and found himself part of an impromptu gathering of colleagues discussing Jack Caswell. Nobody knew what to say. Sue asked if Jack had been seeing a counsellor. Stephen said yes. 'And I took him to lunch.'

Sue frowned. 'Was that wise? There's always a power relation in these things.'

'It was just a chat. He seemed okay these past couple of weeks. Part of the group more. Now this.'

'What about the funeral? Should someone attend?'

'When is it?'

No one knew.

'How are the students taking it?'

'Like it hasn't happened. They're young.'

Stephen leant against the doorframe and wondered if he should have seen the signs. He'd been too pleased with himself. He'd helped Jack to find his voice, but hadn't spoken to him since and now it was too late. The sound of Jack's weeping would haunt him a long while.

Stephen lingered until the meeting broke up. George got up from behind his desk and closed the door. 'What happened?'

Stephen stretched, dragged his mind from one bad thing to the other. 'I punched him on the nose.'

George cheered. 'That's great!' He put his arm around Stephen's shoulders. 'I'm proud of you, my boy!'

Stephen shrugged off George's arm. "I'm not. I can't stand blood.'

George was delighted. 'There was blood?' Full of excitement, he ran his hand through his hair and beamed at Stephen. 'I hope this is a sign of things to come.'

'All the time I was hitting him I knew – well, if I didn't hit him, I'd be hitting her. It was horrible.'

'Does his wife know? That it's Sarah, I mean?'

'Yes. She was in a pretty bad way. And I can't see how he could avoid telling her the truth, looking as he does.'

'What will happen now?'

'She'll forgive him – if he wants to be forgiven. She's that kind of woman. But ... I don't know. She did take great care to invite me round to witness her breakdown.' Stephen told George about Lorna's phantom cooking.

George looked thoughtful. 'Perhaps she didn't know what she was doing. Or sensed she needed someone to stop her going too far. Or – *or* – she might be tougher than you think. She got you to do her dirty work, after all.'

'What do you mean?'

'You punched her husband, brought everything into the open for her. Now all she has to do is pronounce sentence.'

'That hadn't occurred to me.'

'What about you and Sarah?'

Stephen shrugged. 'Who knows? We can't go on as we are. There's Christmas to get through as well. That'll be a farce.'

Stephen contemplated the immediate future with gloom while George smiled from the sidelines. Stephen looked at him. 'I can understand now something poor Jack Caswell told me. Hamlet nursed his grievance for as long as he could because he knew as soon as he actually did something about it his life would be made even more unpleasant.'

'Sometimes we have to go through hell before we find our own kind of paradise.'

'I can't begin to know where to look for my paradise.'

'It'll find you, dear boy. Just wait and see.'

'I have a feeling, George, that I was expelled a long long time ago and it was all my fault.'

That night he heard Emma sobbing into her phone. 'My fucking life, Sammi ... I don't know what to do. Everything's breaking up ... I've got nowhere to go ... Nobody cares – they're all out for themselves ... I wish I could get away from everyone ... Why are people so fucking stupid? ... Oh God ...'

Stephen withdrew and sat in the darkened kitchen. Could Sarah and he spend some kind of Christmas together at Audrey's with Emma, making the best of it for her sake, this one last time? It seemed unlikely. At least they wouldn't have to spend New Year's Eve at Paul and Lorna's. He never had liked their parties.

He thought of Jack's body hanging alone in the dark in his parents' garage.

12

Stephen immersed himself in work. He put in long hours, staying late into the evenings before returning home. It was a distraction and a comfort. He slept in the spare bedroom. Sarah and he led separate lives. She had quickly lost her desire to talk and did not tell him anything.

Gordon Zellaby smiled at him, benign and forgetful. Sue Morse watched him, thoughtful and suspicious. George Ringer congratulated him on his professional renaissance, his new-found appetite for preferment. 'You're really putting it about again like you used to! Ginger's backing towards the ropes. Keep on like this and it's in the bag!'

George continued to assume that Stephen wanted what he wanted. Stephen remained unsure, but he put in the work anyway, sending helpful emails, suggesting initiatives, speaking up at meetings. He took out a couple of pro vice-chancellors to lunch. He presented them with a reasonably logical argument about standards of scholarship and the future of the university, and carefully avoided mentioning Sue Morse and the fact he really couldn't care less.

His weight had stabilized at around sixty-seven kilos. The

pains in his stomach became less frequent. He felt confident enough to visit the doctor, who could find nothing wrong. 'Have you been under much stress these past few months? That could easily be a factor.'

He attended a memorial service for Jack Caswell at a little church in a windswept suburb and surrounded by a crowded graveyard. Nothing that was said seemed to have much connection with the young man he had barely known. There were few people Jack's age among the congregation and no one he recognized from his year. Jack's parents were stony and dignified. Stephen offered his condolences, to which they returned bleak smiles of incomprehension.

Then, one day, he looked at his diary and saw Giuliana's name. They had not communicated since her email about her film, after which he'd received an official invitation from the Italian embassy to attend the screening at a West End cinema. That was as far as it went. He felt disappointed. He'd spoken to Emma of ambassadorial receptions and champagne cocktails with high-ranking diplomats, and if she wanted she could come along. But the invitation made no mention of such splendours and was extended only to him.

'I wish we could go together, but it's just for one,' he told Emma. 'Besides, they sound pretty cheapskate. I'm sorry.'

Emma nodded, said nothing. She had grown sullen and

uncommunicative, keeping to her room when at home, going out as much as she could. Even the rows with her parents had diminished. It felt like nobody cared enough to fight.

'I'll make it up to you, I promise,' Stephen told her, while he remembered there was a great deal to make up for. Where on earth could he begin?

'What the hell's going on?' Audrey asked when he phoned one evening from his office. 'Are you and Sarah just going to stew like that the rest of your lives?'

'I'm just pausing for breath. We both are.'

'Screwing your best friend isn't enough? You need something else?'

He resisted the temptation to remind her of her own infidelity and his father's subsequent faithfulness. 'We're just tired, Mother. We'll work something out.'

'What's to work out? You told me what she did to you. You need to get out of that relationship quick –'

'Quickly.'

'– before it's too late.'

He lost his temper. 'I can handle things, Mother! There's no need –'

'There's every need! She'll walk all over you if you're not careful. Don't give an inch, do you hear?'

'I don't intend to give her anything! You don't know how

things are. Stop telling me what to do.'

She hung up on him. He supposed she was disappointed there'd be one less guest for Christmas, even if it was someone she didn't like.

London turned out to be rain-soaked and despondent behind a bright façade of festive cheer. The early evening crowds barged and elbowed through a mist of rain and frustrated intentions. He was glad to find the cinema and get out of the weather. The bottoms of his trousers were drenched and his socks were wet. He smelled of traffic fumes and fatty aromas.

There were no reserved seats for the ordinary guests, so he sat in the stalls and gazed sightlessly at the big empty screen. He was on his own among all these people and it suited him just fine. A numbing tiredness took a pleasant hold of him. It felt good to work hard. The teaching had been as enjoyable as always. He felt he'd regained respect in the eyes of his colleagues, and that his students liked him. He needed to be liked by someone.

The place filled up. People stood about, leaned over seating, greeted and talked. Most of them were English. He had expected to be cast adrift in an ocean of Italian. He was relieved and disappointed. The warmth of the auditorium stirred him into restlessness. Excitement – or was it nervousness? – took hold of him. He had not yet seen Giuliana and the thought of suddenly doing so ... He wondered what they would have to say to one another after all this time.

She arrived at the last minute. He saw her across the room, amid a group making its way to the front. He recognized her smile before anything else. Her hair was different, a lighter colour than he'd remembered. It was piled on top in a way he associated with her occasional outbursts of temper. She was wearing an elegantly simple dress in maroon and beige with a matching jacket that looked well cut and expensive. He watched her face – its expressions of delight and concern, a questioning frown and a dismissive pout; noticed her full lips and wide mouth, those eyes so deep and serene, and asked himself if she were as unhappy as he.

When she reached her seat she glanced around, her restless gaze darting about, pausing here and there – on Stephen for one startling moment, without seeing him. His heart leapt with something or other, then fell back, tired and forlorn, when she failed to recognize him. No reason why she should.

She turned her back and sat down, reached behind and scratched at her neck. The men beside her talked across to one another and Stephen thought he recognized Tonio, her partner, whom he had never met, but seen that one time in Florence. Was it really him? It had been long ago and far away, that first and only sight of his rival, and his memory had distorted its store of images with years of bitterness.

The lights dimmed, people shushed one another and something approaching silence was almost attained. Stephen braced himself for the usual assault of advertising, but instead here was the film and here was Giuliana's name. And here was her story.

He had never visited Rome and could only identify the obvious: the Colisseum, the Pantheon, the Trevi Fountain from *La Dolce Vita*. The city looked ravishing and sordid, beautiful and ugly, serene and tumultuous. He guessed it was all those things at once. He could not understand a word of dialogue. Lost and bewildered, he was tossed between vague intimations of comprehension and desperate reliance on awkward over-concise subtitles. Gradually, he learned to remove his eyes from the confusing written text and trust his ears and his memory. Slowly, the Italian he'd learned one long hot summer when he was young and full of plans seeped into recollection, and despite the Roman accents, he could begin to grasp the pleasures on offer.

The film was called *Il Grido* – The Cry – and it was a love story of sorts, embedded in a web of storylines spun with intricate care throughout the film. Two hours and ten minutes of delicately wrought drama, written by someone who knew what they were doing and only partially compromised by some uneven direction. Yes, it was a love story all right, Stephen decided. Love used and burned up by the white heat of cowardice. His cowardice. It was his story, and that of Giuliana.

He watched, fascinated, outraged, embarrassed. The darkness of the room spared his blushes. Had he really been like that – had she? He wondered how much he could infer about Giuliana from the character of the young woman, whose inscrutability suggested so much, provoked such longing. She moved through her own life's drama as if she were its author, able to predict but not forestall, trapped in her own desire to make something better than what she was able to give. Snatches of conversation, a scene on a restaurant terrace, unreasoning jealousy – they played out like evocations of a love lost long ago, unable to survive because only she had believed in it.

He had not remembered the rows and the sullen silences. The young man was prone to childish outbursts of anger and naïve enthusiasm, proud boasts of what he would do with his life. It was clear that he did not know himself, had never tested the talents he claimed to possess. He was young and had a lot to learn. Yet he was charming in spite of it and because of it. He had a heart and a brain, but not enough of either.

The lights went up as the credits rolled and the audience clapped. A few people cheered. Stephen remained seated, blinking back his astonishment. Had Giuliana known what she was doing when she wrote this story? Was it for this she had invited him tonight? He could not understand what the film had done to him.

The people on either side were impatient to leave, so he had to stand up and let them by. As he did so, he looked towards Giuliana, but she was gone, swept up by her friends and gone. He might just be able to make the last train home. But home was no longer home. The thought of the journey, then his key in the lock, the closing of the door, Sarah in bed asleep or pretending – these were things he could not face. He made his way to the crowded foyer, saw the darkness waiting for him beyond the bright lights and the rows of doors.

'Stephen!'

He turned and saw Giuliana waving at him. She waited while he weaved through a throng of guests.

'Stephen! You weren't leaving already?'

He smiled. 'I didn't want to, but I thought I'd lost you forever.'

They kissed and hugged like friends. He could smell her perfume, the sweetness in her hair. 'How are you?' he asked. 'You're looking well.'

'I feel well! Life is very good just now. Do you like the film?'

'Yes, I do. I thought it was wonderful. Was it –?'

Giuliana grimaced. 'The director –' she looked over her shoulder – 'the director was not our first choice, but he didn't spoil too much.' She smiled broadly. 'And how are you?'

'I'm delighted to be here, Giuliana.'

She took hold of his arm. 'Are you coming with us?'

'Coming where?'

'There is a party. I thought you understood.'

'You forgot to tell me about the party.'

'Did I?' She frowned. 'I meant to email the details. I must have forgotten.' She laughed. 'But no matter. You are here now. Come on!'

Caught up in her enthusiasm, Stephen laughed and walked with her to a rain-soaked taxi rank. They were accompanied by a crowd of her compatriots, all of whom seemed to know one another and all of whom talked at the same time. 'We're all behaving like typical Italians,' Giuliana laughed. 'Have you noticed? It must be the weather.'

After a long and largely incomprehensible discussion about who should travel with whom, Stephen was told to get in a car and hurry up about it. 'See you in a minute!' Giuliana waved.

Stephen watched the lights float by as he looked out the window of the taxi he shared with two strangers. They did not look happy to have been handed the booby prize. They talked in low tones and used their own language. Stephen could understand them when he supplemented the sounds he heard with some discrete lip-reading.

'Where's the party?' the man asked. He was lugubrious and overweight, wrapped tight in a bulging overcoat. His fleshy face was flushed and moist. He dabbed at his skin with a crumpled handkerchief.

'Some hotel,' said the woman, who might have been his wife. She removed her hand from his knee – no, not his wife, he already had one of those back home – and smoothed out the folds of her fur coat. The aroma of her perfume filled the taxi and mingled with the stale cigarette smoke that clung to her hair. 'I hope there's food. I'm starving.'

The man's mobile whined. He checked the screen, grimaced and put the phone back in his pocket. The woman looked at him, eyebrows raised.

'Guido again. He can wait.'

The woman clicked her tongue, looked with eager despair at the passing streets. 'God! It's so ugly here! How do they stand it?'

'Don't judge by this. London's a great city.'

The woman shivered. 'We'll be home tomorrow, thank God.'

The man looked exasperated. 'You badgered me to come along and now you can't wait to get back. I told you what it would be like.'

'It's so cold.'

'It's winter.'

'But so dreary! You saw those people tonight. Nobody knows how to dress. Everyone looks like the gardener.' She glanced at Stephen. 'Even this guy.'

'Careful!' The man glanced at Stephen, who pretended to watch a passing bus. 'He might catch on.'

The woman looked doubtful. 'Who is he?'

'Some friend of somebody.'

'Everyone's a friend of somebody. Is there anyone who actually does anything around here?'

'You'll see them at the party.' The man looked at Stephen. 'You are a friend of ...?' he asked in English.

'Giuliana. One of the screenwriters.'

The man looked interested. 'Oh, yes, we know Giuliana. And Tonio, of course. My friend – she does not speak English.' They all shook hands. 'You are in the business?'

'No. I'm just an old friend of Giuliana's. Nothing more.'

The man looked puzzled. 'And not of Tonio?'

'No. We've never met.'

The Italian couple exchanged glances, fell silent. A few minutes later the taxi had parked outside bright double doors. The man insisted on paying. 'Expenses,' he explained.

'Molte grazie,' Stephen told him.

A suite of rooms had been reserved at the top of the building. The curtains had been left undrawn so the guests could admire a stunning view of London lit up. Stephen watched the lights and the glitter, at the heart of which was a big patch of darkness that must have been a park. Nothing seemed real. He felt like a spinster at a bachelor party.

He saw Tonio across the room. He was definitely the young man he'd seen in Florence. So Giuliana really had ended up with him. His hair was thinner now, the eyes crafty rather than intelligent. They darted around as he spoke, as if he were covering all the possibilities. Stephen disliked him from a distance and felt sure that things would not improve should he meet him. Giuliana joined Tonio's group for a moment, but they did not look at one another and presently she went away.

Stephen turned back to the window and watched his reflection come and go against the patterns of the city. He felt hungry. He thought of his need for big meals. He had put on a little weight – not much, but he was heading in the right direction. He went to the buffet spread on an L-shaped table and helped himself to as much as he could put on his plate.

He ate alone in a corner and let his eyes moist over with memories – of the time he and Sarah lay in bed while someone knocked at their hotel door; of the first time Emma had smiled at him after he had married her mother; of Giuliana walking through a perfumed garden on a summer's evening. His own presence in these recollected scenes was dim, as if his mind had forgotten to put him inside his own experience – an inessential onlooker. He thought then of Angela's accusation. She'd told him – what was it? – that all he did was float above it all. Was she right? Was it possible to become detached from your own life, despite the feelings you thought you had? He had been a lucky man. Perhaps that was the problem. He'd been educated and encouraged and been given opportunities that others hadn't. Maybe that was what they meant when people like George and Angela accused him of lack of engagement. Had he really turned his back on so much in pursuit of so little? He thought of the film.

The talking and the laughter increased. The room was full. People sat down around him. Somebody put on some music. He heard a woman singing and began to hum along. Good God! His mother! He stood up and looked around to see who on earth had chosen an obscure recording by Audrey Ketley. He looked at people's faces as they talked and drank and ate, shouted and kissed, but it was impossible to tell – the music was on all sides and the room was too crowded, with yet more people arriving.

You need to spend your time with me,

For life is short and love is strong ...

Take the Late Train. The one great studio version she'd made of the song, haunted by the imminent collapse of her life. Her voice was like velvet and sand. She must have sensed that something was up.

And who knows who and what you'll see,

When that late train rolls along? ...

A great ache began in his heart and enclosed him in

melancholy, and he had to turn his back on everyone and pretend to be admiring the view. Poor dear Audrey! He would phone her and tell her she was still appreciated. It would make her day.

He had not expected this.

Then, in the window, he saw Giuliana's face. She was standing at his shoulder, behind him. Their eyes met and he smiled, without turning. She moved forward and stood at his side, their backs to the party. He could smell her perfume, feel the warmth of her body. She held a drink in her hand, her arm crossed over her breast. She smiled suddenly, so that both of them knew it was she who had selected the music.

'Thank you,' he said.

'Tell me about the film,' she replied.

'I don't remember all the rows,' he told her reflection.

'Oh! We had lots!'

'Or being that good looking.'

'You weren't! Only movie stars are that good looking, and then only on screen. You should see him in real life.' She pulled a crazy face, laughed.

Stephen shook his head at her. 'For a reasonably intelligent young man, I certainly had more than my fair share of idiocy and ignorance. I'm surprised you put up with me.'

'I'm surprised *you* could put up with you.'

'Is that why we didn't work out?'

He saw her shrug, her eyes following an aircraft's stately descent. Somebody somewhere dropped a glass on the tiled floor and exclaimed a Roman obscenity. Someone replied, then laughed.

'You were an emotional investment that could not pay off in the short term.' Giuliana smiled an apology. 'The film industry is run by accountants.'

'So you bought shares in Tonio?'

She nodded. 'Which I will sell short.'

Stephen expressed his sympathy. 'I am sorry to hear that.'

'It's been a long time coming.'

'And then what will you do?'

'Work. Work really hard.'

Stephen looked at the darkness in the middle of the city. 'I know what that's like.'

'You do?'

'It helps you find out what you want. What you should have wanted all along.'

'If you're lucky.'

Stephen sighed. 'Life is a completely vague undertaking, it seems to me. That's why we have films like yours, and literature. They give us the illusion of clarity. Like this view.'

It seemed they could not look at one another while they spoke. Something was in the air between them, like the broken filaments of some invisible web they once had weaved but which was long since torn. Stephen found himself thinking of a new beginning with a woman whose beauty and intelligence baffled and intrigued him. He felt the backs of their fingers brush against one another when they shifted position, then again. And then, for one moment, their fingers were clasped, and it felt suddenly as if all those glittering lights amid the darkness made sense with their patterns and their movements, and he could see his life for what it was. Sarah and he had failed, and perhaps never seriously tried, to understand that love was more than what they'd had, even when things were good. He had once known love with the woman at his side, but he had not recognized or valued it, because his youth would not let him and assured him it would come again. It had lied to him.

Someone called, and he felt her fingers stiffen, then leave his hand. She turned and she was swept away by the world. Only this time, he decided, he must not let go so easily.

The party over, he wondered where he could go. The world had become an inhospitable place. He would have to remember that.

'Stay here,' Giuliana told him later when he tried to leave. 'You can sleep on the sofa.'

Stephen said no. 'I've remortgaged my house and can afford a cupboard in some sleazy hotel for the night.'

'There's a lock on my bedroom door. I have a spare toothbrush and there are plenty of towels.'

'What about –?'

'He won't be back this evening. He is not in the habit of returning home after an evening such as this.'

'It's very kind.'

'Of him?'

Her eyes smiled at him. He laughed.

In the morning, when the light was grey and the sound of reversing delivery vehicles woke him up, he took a shower and dressed in a hotel robe. He made coffee and drank it at the window. He heard the sound of the shower, and when Giuliana joined him her hair was still damp.

Sarah felt a long way away.

13

Ella and Billie tore into undergrowth, paws skittering over frozen puddles and copper-coloured leaves – sniffed and worried at the clattering branches of fallen trees – stared with doleful eyes on the frosted landscape while they urinated in tandem behind a moss-covered log.

Emma and her friend Sammi spoke in undertones, their heads together as they skirted a treacherous skein of rutted mud brimming with ice. From a distance they could be mistaken for twins: the same height, the same waist-length hair, the same hooded coats. They even shared a voice – brittle and bright, with the final upward lilt that annoyed Emma's mother.

Stephen hoped it would snow in time for tomorrow. The sky was leaden and full of threat. It was bitterly cold, but the glacial wind of yesterday had blown itself out. He'd borrowed his father's coat again, and found his Wellington boots in one of the sheds. They were a little too large, so he'd put on a couple of pairs of socks, which had already begun to clot around his toes and soon would require pulling up before they fell off.

He called to the hounds when they went into a trance and looked about them as if fallen there from another planet.

Otherwise he kept silence and left the girls to themselves. He knew the way and they were happy to trail him, in and out of earshot, close enough for him to catch their giggles and the occasional helpless laugh.

Every breath – human and canine – rose in a mist and was gone forever. The raw day and the aromas of forest and woodsmoke made Stephen feel clean inside. Yet the cleanness had a melancholy edge. The sound of his boots on the iron-hard ground, the rumble of distant traffic, the hollow echo of the girls' laughter – it all had a valedictory ring, for this was Christmas Eve, and the year was coming to its end. He would not be sorry to be in at the death. Some years stand out like monuments to sorrow and this was one of them.

Angela and Buzz were due to arrive today – nobody knew exactly when. Lunch would be at an indeterminate hour, the dining table decorated and set for six. Audrey had ostentatiously removed the seventh place setting while Stephen looked on, perplexed as to why she should have wanted Sarah there anyway, when it was clear how much she had come to hate her. He supposed, in a way, that he should feel pleased, as it showed his mother was on his side, even though she took his wife's absence as a personal insult. Perhaps she had looked forward to making a scene.

He and the girls had left Audrey and Mrs MacDougall to their joint preparations, as Mrs MacDougall could only stay a couple of hours. Audrey had laid in prodigious stocks of alcohol. She was determined to enjoy herself, no matter what happened with Angela and Buzz. She had welcomed Sammi with the kind of effulgent bonhomie that embarrasses and distresses young people so very much, but the moment had passed and the two girls were content to be left alone. Emma's friend also came from a postmodern family with stepparents and stepchildren and innumerable complexities.

Stephen watched the hounds going about their doggy lives and felt his mind gently close itself to everything except Giuliana. She was back in Rome and he was here in these woods, yet an invisible cord connected them both. He wondered if he dared take a firm grip on the frayed strands that wound around his heart and give that cord a tug. Would it bring them closer together or would it snap? He had hopes, but he could have misread the situation, read into her kindness and friendship and the wonder of her film much more than there was. He had, he realized, misread so much of his life.

And then there was the job.

George had promised to phone him immediately he had learned the outcome of the PVCs' deliberations. In view of Gordon Zellaby's illness, they had agreed to meet this very day to decide on his successor. Stephen calmed his nerves by picturing a secret conclave of chattering PVCs, all clutching glasses of amontillado while discussing the merits of Sue Morse – still the hot favourite as far as Stephen was concerned – and one Stephen Ketley, who had shown no sign of wanting the job until recently. Zellaby would be among them, health permitting, making his key intervention on behalf of Stephen. Gordon's opinion would carry a lot of weight, but exactly how much weight it was hard to say in the circumstances. George would be pacing the corridors outside, along with Sue perhaps, or more likely swigging from a bottle of bitter in his office. Sue would be standing at her office window, saying farewell to the view she detested.

In the last few weeks Stephen had found himself taking a keen but curiously dispassionate interest in the affair.

'You should come along and be seen, Stephen!' George had begged when he learned that Stephen had no intention of returning to an empty university simply to be told he hadn't got the job. 'Last-minute lobbying and all that. Sue is bound to be there, curse her, incorrigible ferret that she is.'

'Sorry George, I think I've done as much as I can bear. I still don't know if I want the bloody job.'

Stephen had come to regard George as a kind of campaign manager, whose advice he took for the most part, yet whose sudden disappearances at key moments had been disconcerting. George had been acting mysteriously of late, his habitual cynical outspokenness reigned in. And he'd done something different with his hair: Stephen had been puzzled about it for days, before realizing that George had simply run a comb through it.

Stephen grasped the phone in his pocket and felt abruptly miserable. He probably didn't want the job, he told himself, yet it would simplify things enormously if his future at the university were secured – wouldn't it? The truth is, he admitted, he didn't know what he wanted. Perhaps Angela was right: he had floated above everything, uninvolved and oblivious to what was going on around him – especially in his marriage. Now he had descended to *terra firma*, only to find himself alone on a darkling plain.

The path forked and he stopped. Emma and Sammi looked tired. When they drew near they both fell silent. 'The long way or the short way?' he asked.

They looked at one another. Sammi gave an indecisive shrug and Emma said she didn't mind.

'The short way then. I could use a drink – only don't tell my mother.'

Light retreated from the day as if absorbed into wood, stone and earth by ineluctable force. When they reached the house at mid-afternoon it seemed as if evening were already upon them. A rusting ruby-red Triumph Spitfire with an empty luggage rack bolted to the boot was parked close to the front door.

'Keep music live,' Emma read out from a sticker on the side

window.

'Nuclear power no thanks,' said Sammi. The girls looked at each other and laughed.

Stephen sighed. The car could only belong to Buzz.

Buzz's furtive emergence from the shadow of a laurel shrub was signalled by a strained and anxious greeting. 'Hey Steve! Good to see you! It's been a long time!' He stared at Sammi. 'And Emma, right? My God you've grown!'

'*I'm* Emma. That's my friend Sammi.'

Buzz kissed the girls and shook Stephen's hand.

'Hello Buzz. Where's Angela?'

Buzz was still admiring Sammi. 'Angela?'

'Your partner. My sister.'

'Yeah, she's in the garden – I think. She had to get out the house.'

'Already? She's only just arrived.'

Buzz shrugged. 'You know how it is, Steve. It's a miracle she made it here at all.'

Stephen scrutinized Buzz and tried hard to discern the youthful prodigy shown in the publicity calendar he had seen in Angela's office. Buzz's hair had begun to thin and he sported a full beard as if to compensate. His shapeless fawn pullover had seen better days, while his jeans were frayed and the toe of his left boot had a hole in it. Stephen wondered about his age – not for the first time, as Buzz had always managed to convey the impression he was younger than he looked. It was years since they last met, but his single-minded attention to the opposite sex was undiminished.

As Buzz was clearly more interested in talking to the girls than in finding Angela, Stephen walked around to the garden and found her standing in the orchard. Stationed beneath an icicled crown of boughs, she was looking out over the valley, which was bluegrey behind a haze of oncoming fog. Lights shone diffuse and yellow from distant windows, while in the town below a dog's bark troubled the surrounding silence.

Stephen stared at her darkening shape and wondered how on earth to tell her she was not his sister. How could he tell someone whose memories were intimately entwined with his own, with whom he had shared a bathroom and a childhood, mealtimes and holidays –games of hide-and-seek in this very garden – that she was not, after all, whom everyone believed her to be? How would it feel to learn that about herself?

Angela turned suddenly and watched him approach. She looked tense, her hands clenched in the pockets of her knee-length coat. 'Merry Christmas Stephen. I wish I'd never bloody well come. This is your fault.'

'Merry Christmas Angela.'

They stared at one another for an awkward moment, then

managed to embrace.

'Audrey told me about you and Sarah.'

'She got that in quick.'

'I think she hopes it's set a precedent – she keeps calling Buzz "Bing". Where *is* Sarah?'

'No idea.'

'Not with your friend – what's his name?'

'Paul. Let's not talk about it. I nearly killed him the other day and ... well ... I hate to think about it.'

'You did? I can't believe it!'

'It's true I assure you.'

Angela looked dubious. 'And what about you and Sarah?' When Stephen shrugged, she said: 'I must admit I never did like her. Still, she'll be relieved she didn't have to come here today. I – Stephen, what on earth are you doing?'

Stephen had felt the tremble of his mobile in an inside pocket and begun to contort his arms inside his coat, whose folds were deep and mysteriously impenetrable. It was a message from George. *No news.* 'I'm waiting to hear about a job,' Stephen explained.

'Oh.' Angela coughed. 'Stephen? Be nice to Buzz, won't you?'

'Of course!' said Stephen, remembering Buzz's predatory interest in the girls when they encountered him behind the bushes. And what exactly had he been smoking? Stephen had thought nothing of it at the time, but now he recalled Buzz's furtive disposal of a homemade cigarette which he'd ground decisively beneath his heel while erecting a diversionary grin on his raddled features. 'How are things between you both?'

Angela shrugged. 'All right. Better than you and Sarah, obviously.'

'I'm glad. What's your secret?'

'Perhaps I'm more tolerant of infidelity than you are.'

'Why do you put up with it, Angela?'

She shrugged her shoulders and crossed her arms over her chest. 'It's who he is. What can I say? I love him and that's who he is. And he loves me.'

'But what if it were the other way around?'

'How do you know it isn't?'

'Well I don't of course ...'

'Things are complicated Stephen. Much more complicated than you think.' Angela shivered. 'Let's go inside. Audrey's overdue for a trip down Memory Lane. She'll want to drag us along with her.'

'Is that really so bad? I've been collating her memorabilia in the attic, trying to make sense of it all ... Angela wait! I have something to tell you. That is, unless you already know.'

Angela turned and gave another shiver. 'Hurry up, I'm cold! What is it?'

'Well, I don't know how to say this ... I thought it would be easy but now ... Audrey let slip something the other day I think you should know.'

Angela immediately looked suspicious. 'What?'

'Well, before I tell you, I want you to know that it makes absolutely no difference – to me that is. You're still my sister and I love you.' Stephen held up his hand when he saw Angela's mouth open in protest. 'I know, I know. But I mean it. And now I want to be more of a brother to you than ever I have been – since we were kids really ...'

'Stephen, I'm *cold*. What is it?'

'Angela ... we're not brother and sister – that is, not strictly speaking. I'm your half-brother.'

Silence.

'Then who –?'

'Your real father was Ronnie Butterman. Audrey's bassist.'

Angela stared at him, her face a blank. He waited for her to speak, to bombard him with questions, to tell him it was a lousy joke. Instead, she turned and walked back to the house, her breath surging into the cold still air.

Stephen, suddenly persuaded he should have let sleeping dogs lie, trailed after her and tripped over an empty guitar case left gaping in the hall. Buzz was tuning up somewhere, the strings plucked irritatingly at random, it seemed, and calculated to annoy anyone within earshot.

'Bing, play a carol!' shouted Stephen's mother.

'Sure Aude.' Silent Night was Buzz's choice for openers.

Stephen found them in the sitting room, Buzz perched on the arm of Audrey's favourite easy chair, bent intimately over his guitar, Audrey herself in dreamy rapture beside the drinks cabinet. She had changed into a long black dress that hung straight down from her shoulders, and she had draped herself with several metres of gold chain and earrings to match. 'Stephen – what the hell's the matter with you?'

'Oh nothing! I was just thinking about something.'

'Have a sherry! Where *is* everyone?'

'I don't know. When are we eating?'

'In half an hour.' Audrey, gold arm bangles clattering, handed him a generous schooner of sherry, then walked to the open door. 'Come on everybody! Let's sing!'

Stephen looked at Buzz, whose unseeing eyes possessed the curious mixture of mental vacuity and acute concentration peculiar to musicians intent on their art. Stephen envied him his private world, which wasn't like the writer's, it seemed to him. Authors' expressions seldom expressed peacefulness, and their frowns of concentration usually contained a liberal dose of panic and deeply felt anxiety.

Audrey began to sing the first verse of Silent Night. Buzz

looked up and smiled.

'Come on Stephen!' Audrey insisted, beckoning him over.

'All right, but only the first verse.'

'The first verse is all I know! We'll have to repeat. Okay Bing, take her away!'

Buzz did not appear to notice he was now named Bing. Perhaps it was the cigarette he'd smoked that made him so mellow. Then Emma and Sammi came in. They both were red in the face and they didn't know where to look. Stephen assumed it was embarrassment. If so, they were in good company. Audrey corralled them into a choir-like crescent formation on the carpet facing the Christmas tree and badgered everyone to sing.

Buzz segued into Good King Wenceslas, then Hark! The Herald Angels. When they'd all had enough, he played a gentle melody no one recognized.

'What's that, Bing?' Audrey demanded from the sofa, her sherry clasped to her chest.

'Something of my own.'

'It's lovely.'

'Not bad. Still unfinished.' He smiled at the girls and didn't look away.

Stephen was worried about Angela and distracted by his phone. Still no news. Then it was time for lunch.

'Where's my daughter? Angela!'

Stephen went upstairs to fetch her and found her on the landing, looking through the fog that clung to the coloured glass of the gothic window. 'Angela, it's time to eat. Are you all right?'

He stood at her side and waited for an answer. She seemed taller, her eyes level with his own; he looked down and saw she was wearing high heels. When she took hold of his arm he felt a thrill of surprise.

'This used to be my favourite place. I'd stand here and shift about so I could see through the different colours. The sky was always blue and those fields we can't see anymore were filled with golden corn. And the trees were green and full of red blossoms. It was the only time I felt safe. Here in my own perfect world of colours.'

Stephen felt a stab of pain and remembrance, so closely conjoined as to be indistinguishable. With the vivid clarity of unappeased heartache, he recalled Sarah's book about the Matisse chapel in Vence, the stained glass window of bitter lemon yellow and aquamarine blue that had ravished him with its innocent joyfulness on the night of his wedding anniversary. How much time had passed since then, with its flotsam of illusions and deceptions, to leave him here, washed up on a lonely strand with no help for his pain.

Not so lonely. He had a family of sorts. Emma. Audrey. And Angela here at his side. He looked at her in the fading light from the window and recalled her words. 'What do you mean, "the only time you felt safe"? What was there to be frightened of?'

Angela turned, suddenly impatient, bitterness etched in lines around her mouth. 'Even *you* must remember my nightmares.'

'Yes, but –'

She stared at him with something like contempt. 'Oh come on, let's get this over with!'

He followed her down to the dining room and saw Buzz draw away from Emma and Sammi, on whom he had evidently been practising his charm. Angela glared at him.

At his mother's command, Stephen opened a couple of bottles of sparkling wine and filled everyone's glasses. Audrey brought in the food. 'Okay everybody, what are you waiting for? Go ahead, eat!'

The dining room echoed with the desultory clatter of cutlery against cracked bone china. Angela, Stephen noticed, was helping herself to the wine almost as much as was Audrey. His sister's eyes were narrowed, and she threw glances at his mother that would have alarmed Audrey had she caught them. Slowly, however, his thoughts turned to his own concerns, while he attended to the conversation with an outward show of wrapt fascination. His phone lay on the table, and he willed it to ring, to vibrate, to play the Trumpet Voluntary if need be, if only it would end this irritant of waiting. The meeting should have been over ages ago. Why hadn't George phoned?

Buzz broke off from an extended chat with Sammi. 'Hey Steve, have you lost weight?'

Buzz was the only person of Stephen's acqaintance who called him Steve. Not since his teenage years had anyone shortened his name. He'd always made it abundantly clear that he hated it. Buzz alone had paid no attention. Suddenly, Audrey calling him Bing seemed to serve him right.

'I have a little, *Bing*, yes.'

Angela looked at him and frowned. Stephen immediately felt guilty. She had received a shock from him and here he was picking on her partner. Buzz, however, took it in his stride. 'I thought so. You look a little – odd.'

'Yes, so I gather.'

Audrey intervened. 'Stephen's been through a lot lately. That bloody Sarah's a two-timing bitch – sorry, Emma, we have to face the truth – which is why my son is here alone today. It's his personal tragedy, but in my opinion he's well rid of her. We all know this and now there's an end to it: we're here to enjoy ourselves *en famille* as the Italians say. Stephen! Would you *please* stop looking at that phone?'

'Sorry, I can't seem to help it.'

'You told me you didn't care about the damned job!'

'I don't – at least, I don't think I do. I just wish I knew, that's all.'

Angela slurped at her wine, spilling some down her front. She didn't notice. 'You don't belong there Stephen! Tell them what they can do with their job! What the hell's a pro vice-chancellor anyway? Just a glorified clerk! That's no job for my brother – my dear *departed* brother!'

Sammi giggled and looked down at her plate. Emma fidgeted under the table. Buzz winked at them both.

Audrey held up her glass. 'Choices, Stephen! Here's to the right choice.'

'There may not be a choice, Mother.'

'There's *always* a choice. Look at me! I've had to make choices – pretty tough choices.'

'And invariably the wrong ones.'

Audrey stared at him, then laughed. It was so unexpected that everyone else joined in. Only Angela was unamused. 'Mother has a gift for making the wrong choices,' she announced. 'Wouldn't you say so Brother?'

Buzz stood up.

'Where do you think you're going?' Audrey asked.

'We're out of wine and I thought –'

'That's okay then – there's more in the fridge. Oh Bing? Put some music on while you're out there will you? I'll leave it up to you, but if it isn't one of my albums I'll want to know why. You all right, girls?'

Sammi nodded while Emma smiled.

'Emma! I can't believe you'll be off to university. You don't seem old enough.'

'I might not go straight away.'

'Oh?'

'I thought I'd take a year off.'

'I bet I can guess what your mother said to that bright idea.'

'She didn't like it. Stephen did, didn't you Stephen?'

'What? Oh yes, kind of.'

'And what are your plans Sammi?' asked Audrey.

'I'm not sure. I may go straight to university or I might take a year off as well? Same as Emma?'

'Really?' Audrey gave them both an appraising look over the rim of her empty wine glass. 'What do you make of that, Stephen? Sammi here wants to stay with Emma. Did you hear?'

'I heard.' Stephen spoke to Angela. 'Buzz will be disappointed.'

A piano chord echoed from the sitting room.

'Audrey Ketley Takes the Late Train!' shouted Audrey. 'Great choice Bing!'

Everyone fell silent and listened to the opening bars of No Heart for Loving. Stephen glanced at Angela. Zinc's bass was clearly audible in the background. Midway through the track it would break out in a solo spot famous for its complexity and daring. Stephen asked himself what he would be thinking now if he were his sister – half-sister.

'This was everybody's finest hour,' Audrey told them, humming along to her own voice. 'Your father never wrote anything better than this. And we never performed any better. This is as close to perfection as we can get on this Earth.'

Buzz returned with two more bottles. His eyes looked moist and he kept catching his breath. 'This is really cool, Aude, and I don't just mean the wine.'

'Thanks Bing.'

Buzz went round filling glasses, leaving the girls until last. He rested his hand on their shoulders while he poured for them. When they glanced at one another, Sammi pulled a face indicative of mild disgust.

Stephen's head was foggy with wine and worry. George had still not phoned, Audrey was well on the way to inebriation and Angela was full of dark glances. Buzz was making his usual instinctive moves on the two young women and even the greyhounds looked grim. They'd clipped in together and hung around the table until Audrey had sent them to their beds, where they looked at everyone accusingly.

By the time lunch had dragged to a close, night had fallen. Stephen turned on the lights and pulled the curtains. Emma and

Sammi smiled at one another and volunteered to wash the dishes. They looked relieved to go. The rest of them plodded to the sitting room, Buzz casting wistful looks towards the kitchen. 'Do you think they need any help in there?'

'Sit down Buzz,' Angela told him.

'We had *voices* then!' exclaimed Audrey.

Angela smirked at Stephen.

Audrey was looking at the ceiling, her ears attuned to the music. 'These days nobody sings: they just yell into a microphone and producers take care of the rest. Plus we were adults performing for adults. Jim didn't write one song that – it's all teenage whining about God knows what and who could care less ...'

'Folk,' said Buzz, 'doesn't have that problem.'

'It doesn't have an audience either! You'll never get anywhere singing that crap Bing! Who wants songs about dead fishermen and their grieving kin? It's too depressing!'

'I think there's more to it than that, Audrey,' Stephen told her.

'You teach English, what do you know?'

'Steve's right, Aude. Folk goes in all directions now. Some of it's even a little like jazz. I like your stuff. It's great.'

'Bing, you're okay! I can't say I like your morals, but you know about music.'

'After all, that's what really counts,' said Angela.

'My morals?' Buzz sounded surprised.

'Don't ask,' said Stephen, taking out his phone.

'You've got to clean up your act, Bing! No more tomcatting around. No wonder ... Stephen! Put that damned phone away!'

'No wonder what, Mother Dear?' asked Angela.

'I lost my train of thought ...' Audrey held out her empty glass for Buzz to pour another.

'Now that we're chatting here so agreeably,' Angela said, holding out her own glass, 'it's made me realize what we've been missing all these years.'

'What *you've* been missing young lady.'

'The bottle's empty,' Buzz announced. 'I'll go get another from the kitchen.'

'Sit down Buzz. Stephen can go.'

'All right, as long as nobody says anything nice while I'm away.'

'There's very little chance of that, surely?'

'Turn the record over while you're out there Stephen!'

Out in the hall, Stephen veered left and climbed the stairs to the first landing, where he phoned George.

'Hello?'

'Stephen here George. Is there any – what's going on? It sounds like a party.'

'Oh ... nothing old boy, just the neighbours. Listen, Stephen, I can't tell you anything at present.'

'My God, are they still in their bloody meeting? Do they know it's Christmas?'

'I say! Isn't that a song or something? I thought I heard –'

'George!'

'Don't *worry*, old boy. Things are ... delicate at this stage. Now I really must ring off. Don't call me again. Cheerio. Oh and happy Christmas!'

'George! –'

Stephen, perplexed, stared at his phone. Then he sat down on the top stair and rested his head in his hands. How could life go so wrong? He groped for an answer, but his stomach hurt. Maybe he wasn't asking the right question. Maybe he had never asked the right question.

He turned over Audrey's record on his way to the kitchen. The music pursued him as he padded down the hallway.

What have you been up to while I've been away?

Who said you could love another in the same old way?

'How are you two getting on out here?' he called as he pushed open the kitchen door. He found Sammi and Emma together at the kitchen sink, Emma holding a washing-up brush in one hand, Sammi with a lank tea towel hanging from her arm. She gave a cry like a frightened guinea pig and leapt away from Emma, who turned her back on Stephen and bent low over a stack of dirty plates.

Stephen blinked at them, saw Sammi's beetroot face, Emma's nervous backward glance. 'I ... er ... Sorry!' he said. Then: 'I ... er ... didn't mean to startle you. I'm only here for the wine.' He looked around, felt himself blushing and turned his back. 'I wonder where it is?' He walked to the fridge and retrieved the last bottle of white. He opened it at the kitchen table. 'Thanks for taking care of this, you two ... it's very kind ... although you're not missing much out there, that's for sure. Would you like another glass while I'm here?'

Sammi shook her head.

'Okay then – I'll er ... see you later.'

'Stephen!'

'Yes Emma?'

'Please don't ... I mean ...'

'Emma!' Sammi hissed.

'What?'

'Don't!'

There followed a charged silence while the girls glanced at each other, at Stephen, at the floor. Love, he thought, should never require apology or explanation. The ridiculousness of his own situation assailed him. 'No need to worry, dears,' Stephen told them. 'My lips are sealed.'

He paused outside the kitchen door, his eyes wide with

astonishment. It had even crossed his mind to introduce Jack Caswell to Emma, he remembered. If they had met, would it have changed the course of history and prevented Jack's death? Lives can turn on such trifles. It would only have taken a little effort ... Stephen blinked away a tear, then took a mouthful of wine direct from the bottle.

Voices were raised in the sitting room – Angela and Audrey. He had only been gone a few minutes and already they were fighting. He arrived at a moment of dangerous silence. Audrey's relaxed sprawl, her head at an angle against the cushions propped behind her head, signified an imminent explosion. What was worse, she was playing with the bangles on her drinking arm, metaphorically rolling up her sleeves and ready for a fight. Angela sat tense and erect, nursing an unappeasable grievance. It was as if she had never been away, the hiatus of years annihilated in an instant. Buzz was the only relaxed one among them, his legs extended and crossed at the ankles, his head and hands keeping time with the music.

'This is the last bottle!' announced Stephen, as cheerily as he could. He gave everyone a refill, then sat on the sofa next to Buzz.

'It's good we're all together at long last,' Audrey announced, staring at her daughter. 'Your father would have approved. God I wish he was here with us! This is the kind of Christmas he enjoyed ...'

'And seldom experienced,' muttered Stephen.

'... his family around him, this house, his own music ... I remember one time we had the whole band with us. We'd stopped over for the night on our way somewhere or other – I forget where. That old rickety bus we used was on its last wheels. I didn't think we'd make it home, but we did. Jim had already gone to bed, but we rousted him out and played music till the early hours. I can remember the smell of those cigars Ray smoked, and how Paris always made a show of standing as far away as he could. Geoff and Jim took turns at the piano. I sang. Funny, I always thought I sounded best without a microphone, here in this house.' She looked at Angela and Stephen, made a vague gesture with her free hand. 'You two kids were too young to remember.'

Stephen forgot himself. 'I remember Zinc sitting at the kitchen table and wearing a red dressing gown one morning. He let me carry his double bass until I nearly fell over with it.'

Audrey stared at him. 'That must have been a different time. When your father wasn't around.'

'Whose father do you mean, Audrey? Stephen's or mine?'

Silence.

Buzz looked at Angela. 'What's that Ange?'

Angela feigned surprise. 'Didn't you know? It seems I am not the fruit of Gorgeous Jim's loins after all. Tell him Mother! You like to reminisce. Tell Bing all about it!'

'Angela,' began Stephen, 'let's all try –'

'That's a damned lie!' shouted Audrey. 'Who's been telling – Stephen! What the hell have you been saying?'

'Yeah, what's going on Steve?'

Angela got to her feet and stood over Audrey. 'Look at me! It's me who's talking, not my half-brother. Look at me! Tell us it isn't true!'

'Of course it isn't true! Not *really* true.'

'What the hell does that mean? Either it's true or it isn't!'

Audrey's frown expressed anger and perplexity in equal measure.

'Angela –'

'Shut up Stephen! I'm speaking to your mother.'

'She's your mother too.'

'That's right Ange.'

Audrey lurched to one side and got to her feet. She pointed at Angela, her finger wagging. 'You are my daughter! We always loved you! We ... I couldn't really be sure – things were complicated ... I told Jim and he believed it. I got to believing it too. It was right about then I had my troubles ... Jim was so damned *needy*. You don't know ... He was drowning me in it. I couldn't breathe, couldn't move beneath that suffocating need of his. He was dying inside and expected me to die along with him.

I'll be damned if I do that for anyone!'

Angela stared at her mother. 'Stephen! You told me –'

'I can only tell you what Audrey said to herself one night. I believe it was the truth. She had forgotten I was there and had no reason to lie. Angela, what's the point of this? She'll never confess anything she doesn't want to. You know what a nightmare that time was for her.'

'Nightmare for her? What about *my* nightmares? None of you ever cared about me! The sound of his footsteps on the stairs, the way the landing creaked at night when you had gone to bed ...'

'Ange! Calm down! There's no point in ... Look at her! Aude can't hear you.'

Audrey had fallen back into her chair, her averted face half-concealed by a cushion, her eyes closed.

'She never has heard me! None of you have!'

'Ange!'

'Oh leave me alone!'

Stephen watched his sister leave the room, heard her footsteps on the stairs. He sat back and sighed. The record had finished. 'The rest is silence.'

Audrey was now definitely asleep and gently snoring.

Buzz reached for the wine bottle and shook it. 'Drink Steve? There's a drop left.'

'Hmnn? Oh thanks Bing.'

They clinked glasses. 'Merry Christmas.'

Buzz looked thoughtful. 'Steve ... I don't know if all that's true ... Your sister ... Ange ... well, she has dreams, Steve, always has ... it's not ... I mean it *could* be ... and they go *way* back ... who knows really? The past ... and she's okay now ... you see ... I mean ... there's no physical sign ... who can say? ... mentally is another ... and if that's the ... you know?'

Stephen held his glass to his brow, tried to make sense of Buzz's drunken inarticulacy. It didn't help that there was a jumble of words inside his own head. 'Even so ... I'll talk to her. I must apologize. And listen. Someone needs to.'

'That's nice ... God that's nice! She'll appreciate it. She always missed you Steve.'

'I missed her. I just didn't know it.'

'We all have our demons, Steve ... you ... me ... Aude.'

Stephen looked at Buzz and felt a wave of affection for him that he, Stephen, knew would evaporate by morning. He put a hand on his shoulder and dared to be sincere. 'Audrey was right about one thing Bing: you need to stop chasing women. Especially women half your age. Be a man, Bing. You've got it in you somewhere.'

Buzz fell back in his seat and sighed. 'Life is complicated ...'

Stephen agreed. He finished his wine and suddenly felt tired.

When he awoke, he found himself with his head on Buzz's

shoulder. Buzz was asleep, his mouth open, his hands held loose at his sides. The contents of his wine glass had spilled into his lap. He looked like a withered hirsute child who had wet himself. Stephen retrieved Buzz's glass and put it safely on the table, where his mobile phone was shimmying across Audrey's album cover. He picked it up and answered.

'Stephen! – Sue! I expect you're feeling jolly pleased with yourself. George really pulled a fast one. But of course you know all about that.'

'Do I?' Stephen ran his free hand over his chin, which felt in need of a shave. He was exhausted and his eyes ached as if he had been reading for too long. 'What do you mean?'

'Please! Stephen, give me credit for some intelligence! I know the game you two – you *three* – have been playing. It's pretty despicable whichever way you look at it.'

'Sue, believe me, I have no idea what you're talking about. Do you mean I ... that you didn't get the job?'

'Of course I didn't! Zellaby's so called statement has seen to that, together with his wife's machinations.'

'Machinations?'

'It was beautifully done I must say! While you and I ran around in ever-decreasing circles, the lovely Anthea – so cool, so *very* cool – was calmly pouring honey into eagerly receptive ears. Then when she read out Gordon's declaration it was the *coup de grâce*.'

Buzz shifted position, his head falling across Stephen's arm so that he nearly dropped the phone.

'So they've given the job to me have they?'

'Stephen you're a bloody fool! Of course not!'

'Well, if you didn't get the job and I didn't, who –'

'George, you idiot! George!'

'*George?*'

Stephen dropped the phone in his lap. Buzz leaned heavily against him and began to snore. Emma and Sammi appeared from the kitchen. 'All finished!'

They stared at Stephen, who could hear laughter somewhere far away – uninhibited laughter, great, billowing Falstaffian laughter, a laughter expressive of acceptance and defeat and wisdom and victory, infectious and booming, red-faced and tearful. It was coming closer and closer; so close now that it was inside him. Then Buzz tipped over and fell to the floor and Stephen laughed at him as well, until his stomach ached with laughing, and his tears had soaked his shirt.

'Stephen!' Emma was laughing too, and Sammi, the whole world ...

'I know now ...' he gasped, '... why ... *why* he killed him off!'

'Who?'

'Hamlet! He died – he *died* in the nick of time!'

14

Ping.

Stephen awoke, yawning discreetly. He felt – was convinced – he had dreamed. Frowning, he struggled to retrieve the dream, but already it was fading ... fading ... and now gone, barged to oblivion by the encroaching thighs of the grossly obese teenager floundering next to him.

Annoyed with himself, he fastened his seatbelt and looked out the window. A bank of cloud rose to meet him, shrouded the wing in a bedraggled fleece, drifted overhead. The aircraft tilted; sunlight ebbed on the blazing horizon. His steady gaze took possession of a chequered landscape spliced with silver ribbons, forest-green shadows rising and falling in its intricate folds.

At Pisa, he took the late train to Florence and found a cab at the station. Dusk became night as the car wound through the city. He glimpsed historic buildings illuminated like stage flats, deprived of depth, their façades etched in yellow light, black windows gripped between jaws of monumental stone.

He ate dinner alone at his hotel. The night was hot – too hot for sleep. Through his open window there came the sound of people talking on the street below, their footsteps clipping in rhythm to distant rock music from a loudspeaker outside a bar. Scooters whined and fizzed along narrow roads that ran between high walls. There was a distinct odour of drains.

He lay in his broad wooden bed and stared at a triangle of light cast by a streetlamp on the ochre ceiling. His work in progress – a new book on Edith Wharton – passed in a procession of succinct chapters upon his inward eye. He would need to establish a routine over the coming weeks: a nourishing breakfast; a walk to the library; slow, careful study in panelled rooms lined with venerable books. He would achieve his scholarly objectives.

But first Emma, who would arrive in two days' time for a short holiday. He looked forward to her visit after however many months it had been, pleased she had allotted him time from her summer vacation. He hoped ... that's to say ... of course ...

Stephen floated out of mind on a wave of heat into a dreamless sleep.

The next morning, ignoring the night's resolutions, he decided to take a walk. He would wander, nothing more, and forget schedules and itineraries, the urge to see everything and experience nothing. Better just to wander. Atmosphere is the thing.

The heat was oppressive, with no breeze. He wore cotton trousers and a faded linen shirt that once had been a vivid yellow;

sunglasses and a cheap panama hat. He strolled for an hour, disposed to admire and to savour, pausing delightedly before an elaborate set of iron gates behind which a verdant herb garden nursed a fountain of gently pulsing water.

Then, abruptly tired, he sat outside a bar in a sidestreet and took morning coffee in the shade of a parasol.

He thought about his novel, wondered if he'd ever manage to write it. Compared with the Wharton project it was little more than a suggestion – a boat, the Tropics, the darkening shadows of history. The main thing, he told himself, was finding a beginning and an end: stories are supposed to start and stop, whereas real life ... He frowned, willing his imagination to snap to attention. His mind refused to cooperate. He shook his head and gave it up. Anyway, he reflected, beginnings and endings to stories are more or less arbitrary. Finish the Wharton, then see about the novel.

In a listless mood of distraction, he lingered beneath his parasol and ordered another coffee. He watched the world go by, followed the sun's steady progress across the narrow street. He had always been a watcher, an appreciator of sets, and hence, in a way, an arranger – maybe that was why he was good at his job. What was teaching if not the arrangement of people inside neat little boxes? And his own family – the semblance of happiness by cajoling them into tidy smiling groups?

He checked his watch before walking the long narrow street

to Santa Croce. Tired again, and overheated, he climbed the steps to the entrance, past squatting beggars with glittering gimlet eyes. Inside, he looked up at the ceiling, admired the compartments of frescoes formed by each tastelessly furnished chapel. He sought out the Giottos, remembered *A Room with a View*, wondered why life viewed through another's lens seems more real than seeing it for oneself.

Pushing through the door from the cool interior of the church, he was struck blind by the midday sun, his hands searching frantically for his sunglasses. Afterwards, he walked across the piazza and stood at the exact same spot where he'd watched Giuliana, dressed all in white and waving, all those years ago. The memory drove him back to his hotel.

Emma met him there the next morning, in time to share his breakfast. She entered the dining room and lingered at the threshold, her eyes seeking him out among the crowded tables. He saw her first and waved, proud of her prettiness, of the admiring glances of the other guests, of the evident fact that his stepdaughter was flourishing at university. Physically, she seemed changed in subtle ways he could not identify, and he frowned at her, puzzled. He stood up and waved again. Then, as he watched her sway towards him, it was as if a wave of electricity passed over his body. Emma, he saw, was now fully woman, her glad smile bereft of adolescent inhibition and entirely unselfconscious. Only her perfume – overdone as ever – could remind him of the child he had known: he inhaled deeply.

He poured her a coffee while she made herself comfortable, her blue cotton dress bathed in the morning sunshine that fell through the gauzy curtains at the window. She looked up at the vaulted ceiling, at the dark oil paintings of Renaissance Florentines, at the elderly lady dressed in black who was cleaning the fronds of an aloof-looking palm that stood in the crook of a piano. Cutlery clinked and voices hummed; traffic thundered three floors below.

'What's wrong?' she asked. 'You look nervous.'

Stephen smiled. 'As a matter of fact I am. I've worked out that this room is in the big arch that straddles the road – you must have seen it when you arrived. Which means beneath this floor there's a yawning void of around ninety feet. Is it safe? You're an engineer – reassure me.'

She frowned, took his question seriously. 'A keystone arch is one of the strongest structures ever invented.' Her hands shaped the configuration of stones geometrically arranged to maximize their load-bearing capacity. 'You only have to worry if the keystone starts to vibrate – that's the big stone at the top that holds all the *voussoirs* in place.'

Stephen nodded in understanding, admiration. 'But that's just it, you see. How do they *know* it isn't vibrating?'

Emma sipped her coffee, took care to replace her cup in its saucer before she answered. 'Because if it did, the consequences would be too horrific to contemplate.' She pursed her lips, watched his face express his dismay. Then she laughed. 'Don't worry! All these things are monitored. Signs manifest themselves before things become dangerous.'

'I hope so!' he told her, half-joking.

In sensing that her voice had changed – a little deeper, less emphatic in its final upward lilt – he wondered how he appeared to her. Had he also changed? He'd certainly replaced all the weight he'd lost. He slipped a thumb inside his waistband – and possibly added a little extra.

Emma leant towards him, eyes open wide. 'I have to tell you something,' she stage-whispered. 'You won't believe it!'

Intrigued, he bent towards her. 'I'm all ears.'

'*I* can hardly believe it.'

'What is it?'

'Well, it's about Sarah.'

'Oh!'

He tried to hide his shock. Sarah's name still had the power to make him angry and ashamed, afraid and defeated. He supposed it would always be like that, his mind a sensitive tissue, easily bruised.

Emma paused, waited for him to collect himself. 'I think Mum and Dad might be getting back together.'

'Good God!'

She held out a hand, palm downwards, by way of disclaimer. 'I don't know for sure. But they've been seeing each other – *if* you know what I mean.' She raised her eyebrows and sat back.

Stephen stared at her, his heart beating at his chest. 'I'm amazed! I don't ... How do you feel about it?'

Emma shrugged. 'Kind of pleased and kind of horrified. It's what Dad's wanted all along.'

'You think so?' For something to do, to catch his breath, Stephen helped them both to another croissant. 'He had a string of women in the meantime.'

Emma spooned apricot jam on her plate. 'None of them ever worked out. He never got over you and Mum.'

Stephen thought about that. He watched her lift a strand of hair and tuck it behind her ear. 'Emma? Do you blame me for anything? I mean, should I be feeling guilty about something? If so ...'

She brushed crumbs from her lap and stared pensively at the tablecloth. 'There's one thing.'

'Oh?'

'You never took me to the circus when I was a little girl. You promised but you never did. It's the one thing I've never been able to forgive.'

He laughed in relief. 'I'm sorry! I suppose it's too late now?'

'Far too late. I'll hold a grudge for the rest of my life.'

They smiled at one another, fell pensive. A comfortable silence established itself. 'Do you see much of your parents?' he asked. 'It must be pretty odd for you all.'

Emma pulled a face. 'I try to keep out their way. It's not as if I ever saw much of them anyway. I spent more time with you than anyone. Plus, after all that's happened – well, I can't believe anything is ever permanent. People act as if something is forever but it never is.'

'Yet we still keep looking for it – permanency. I don't think we have any choice. We couldn't go into something without the hope that it'll last a lifetime. Or are things different these days? People your age seem much more casual about relationships and love and ... Or maybe it just looks that way because I'm getting old and jealous.'

Emma shrugged and looked away.

He had, he supposed, unintentionally hit a nerve. Sammi had faded out of the picture – so he assumed, as he never liked to ask. On previous visits, Emma had with her a young man. Stephen had forgotten his name. Something about his diffidence had reminded Stephen of the student who died.

Stephen slowly shook his head. So Andrew and Sarah had turned full circle – he could hardly believe it. He tried to feel pleased for Andrew, who'd finally got what he wanted, yet surely Sarah's return was nothing more than shrewd calculation? She'd thrown away two marriages and lost Paul to Lorna. She was beginning to run out of options. He knew what that felt like.

Emma looked thoughtful. 'I don't know,' she told him. 'Perhaps everything is always in a mess no matter who you are or even *when* you are – look at Audrey. She's virtually my grandma, yet her life ... ' She scrutinized Stephen. 'What about you? Are you really here just to work?'

Stephen was startled. 'What do you mean?'

'Oh nothing! I just wondered if you'd made any arrangements, that's all. You *are* in Florence – where it all started – and you said you'd been seeing Giuliana.'

'*Seeing* her, yes. We Facetimed a few months ago before I came out here ... anyway she lives in Rome now.'

'And that's *so* hard to get to from here.'

'Yes.'

He didn't like to admit the truth – that he was scared. Rome was out of the question because it frightened him what he might find there. Not everything turns full circle and we're not all destined to arrive at a happy ending. He'd said as much to his students before the end of term – appropriately, as it turned out, with regard to *Much Ado About Nothing*. 'Shakespeare,' he'd told them, 'takes care to show us that the cost of happiness for some is paid in the sorrow of others. There is always someone who stands outside the charmed circle of felicity.'

'How's the book?' asked Emma.

Stephen brightened. 'Which one?'

'There's two?'

'I thought I'd told you. Another on Edith Wharton and also – well – I've started to think about a novel.'

He waited for her reaction. She was unimpressed. 'You started to think about a novel six months ago. I remember because Angela took us out for lunch that day.'

'Well, these things take time ...'

'You're telling me! It's about time you wrote something. Noah Tredwell –'

'Noah Tredwell's talent borders on genius; my own, such as it is, merges into mediocrity.'

'What if one of your students said she was *thinking* about writing an essay –'

'All right! I'll start today, I promise.'

'And have you seen her since?'

'Who?'

'Your sister!'

'No.'

'You should. She needs sorting out.'

'I know. Things are complicated ...' Stephen looked up from

the table, frowning playfully. 'Ever since you've grown up you've become a right bossy-boots, do you know that?'

Emma smirked at him. 'It's funny though, isn't it? Who'd have thought they'd still be together – Angela and Bing, I mean?'

'Don't you start calling him that as well.'

Emma laughed. 'He can't hear.' She looked at her watch. 'I mustn't miss my train.'

'Where to today?'

'Pisa. There's a certain leaning tower, apparently, which provides interesting challenges for the engineer.'

'More importantly, there's a great little trattoria round the corner from there which does the best risotto I have ever eaten in my life. Unfortunately, I can't remember where it is, so you'll have to find it yourself. It's literally on a corner –'

'I'll be all right, don't worry.' She looked again at her watch, then stretched her arms above her head. 'I'd better go,' she told him, suppressing a yawn. 'If I were you I'd give Giuliana a call.'

'No. I can't, not yet. Another time.'

'There might not be another time! What are you waiting for?'

'The nerve.'

'Nerve!'

'Giuliana is formidably accomplished, extremely active and terribly attractive –'

'Exactly! You have to move fast! If – oh look, I have to go.'

Emma stood up, smoothed the front of her dress. She waited for him to join her, then grasped his hands. 'Stephen, you can't sit around and wait for her to fall into your lap – so to speak!' She kissed him goodbye. 'Wisdom is wasted on the middle aged!'

'Who are you calling middle aged?'

She kept hold of his hands and gazed into his eyes. A long moment passed, while her face flickered with concern. It was as if she had seen something – an absence of some kind. He lacked, he felt obscurely, a vital extra element of volition and hope. It had been torn out of him, and the missing piece made him pathetically incomplete, an object of her pity. She turned quickly, waved goodbye without a backward glance. The doors closed behind her and she was gone.

He sat down and poured himself the last of the coffee. Emma could not understand that he wished to be by himself for a while. He had to find his own contentment before he could hope to discover it with anyone else.

That afternoon, however, something stirred within him. He looked at maps and made plans and decided on a journey.

The rattling bus climbed out of the bowl of the city and wound into the Tuscan countryside. Sunlight struck at him through the begrimed window. Deposited next to a dusty petrol station on the side of a hill, he started to walk.

He paused at a crossroads, unsure of the way. There used to

be an open field above the villa, with a belt of poplars that shimmered in the upland breeze. If he could find those trees ... He chose the right-hand fork, which led uphill through vineyards with ramshackle stone shelters and the occasional olive tree. The sun was pitiless. He kept going until he saw a belt of trees in the distance. Then, as he crested the hill, the red tiles of a gabled roof appeared to his left, where the ground sloped away. He turned into the field and followed its perimeter until he encountered a low stone wall.

And there it was: the past displayed for his contemplation.

Everything – the house, the garden, the flickering horizon – looked different in subtle ways he could not differentiate. It was as if someone had moved around the furniture of his memory to confound him. Then he realized that it was he who had changed and not his surroundings. The garden was not as expansive or as private as he had pictured it; the house was modest in comparison with his daydreams – and a little run down. It needed painting. A garage door was hanging off its hinges. And the terrace where ... The terrace was hidden behind the house. His eyes followed the road that led past the open gate to the property. If he took that road he'd be able to see the back of the house.

He tramped the hot asphalt that curved downwards along the slope of the hill. While he did so, he thought of Giuliana as he had seen her at the premiere of her film. He remembered the thrill of recognition across the crowded foyer, the touch of her hand at the party afterwards. And her film itself – that love letter to the past and to him. He, Stephen Ketley, had inspired love from which he had run away because he had been too young and too stupid to accept it. He thought it would come again, that Time was on his side. He had been wrong.

The terrace hove into view. That, too, was smaller than he remembered, unmagnified by love.

Stephen breathed deeply and closed his eyes. The pungent aroma of rosemary wafted over him; the hot breeze fluttered at his eyelids. He used to sit at a mosaic-topped table in the shade of a tree whose name he had never known. There, he had typed his thesis and read his books. Giuliana worked part-time at a newspaper even then. He used to check his watch and have lunch ready for her. Their afternoons had been long and lazy with love.

He stood for many minutes and thought how appropriate it would be to end his novel thus, poised between past and present, love and loneliness. Perhaps to stand at the very fulcrum of one's life, where feelings balance in soothing equilibrium, is the best one can hope for in this world.

A car approached on the road at the top of the hill; its gears graunched as it turned and descended.

On the other hand, could he not open his eyes and conjure her presence from the rumble and crunch of tires over gravel ... the clunk of car doors ... a tender cry of surprise and wonder?

'Stephen! Caro! Amore mio!'

He opens his eyes ...

THE END

Thank you for reading Take the Late Train. If you enjoyed it, won't you please take a moment to leave a review at your favourite retailer?

Thank you!

Jack Messenger

Interview with the Author

When did you first start writing?
I've written since childhood, but in recent years it has become my main work. I have published quite a bit of non-fiction, but now I want to tell stories. I believe strongly that in this extremely troubled world of ours, the stories we tell one another really matter. We need to understand one another, to have compassion and empathy. Good fiction helps us in all these things. Fortunately, reading and writing are also very enjoyable.

What is your writing process?
Usually, some kind of idea comes to me for a situation or a line of dialogue – even just a location – and it settles into the back of my mind until I am able to amplify it by thinking of a story. A great deal of a writer's work is done long before the business of typing words commences. I have to live with my ideas a long time before they feel natural and possess enough energy for me to be confident I can do something with them. I've had so many false

starts with things that I haven't really thought through that I have become very cautious: I don't start writing until I'm absolutely sure I'm not wasting my time with a half-baked idea that doesn't work. Once I do start writing, the main thing for me is to find the characters – find their voices and their lives – and then have them interact within a larger context. That's all about giving a shape to the narrative and making the milieu as real and tangible as possible for my readers.

What is the greatest joy of writing for you?

Finishing! Writing is such hard work, and a novel is a real marathon. So I am always relieved to get to the end of a project, having done the best that I can. The pursuit of excellence in writing is never ending. Readers deserve the best you can do and I would not be happy if I did not think I could give of my best. Aside from finishing, I love finding the right words – in dialogue, in descriptions. Language is so beautiful and so complex that finding just the right word, then combining it with other words just as carefully chosen, is a painstaking process of trial and error. Sometimes it's as if I have to force the language to say precisely what I mean. Another great joy is when characters come alive and start to behave in ways I do not expect: it is as if they are in charge of what's happening, not me.

What motivated you to become an independent author?
It seems the ideal opportunity to find readers without having to seek someone's permission or approval beforehand. Today, for a whole host of reasons, mainstream publishing is tremendously averse to taking risks, especially with untried authors, and it is hard for writers even to find someone willing to read their work in order to assess if it is publishable. This is extremely frustrating. So I decided to become an independent author.

What's the story behind your latest book?
Take the Late Train is primarily about a good, intelligent man whose life took a wrong turn when he was young. It describes the unravelling of that life as he grows in self-awareness and self-agency. The writing is peppered with literary allusions, some of which are obvious, others of which are not. I thought these should reflect Stephen's literary preoccupations and tastes, but also illuminate and obscure reality for him.

What are you working on next?
I'm currently working on a novel entitled *The Long Voyage Home*, which is set in the late 1930s. This is much more of an experiment in style than my previous work.

What do you read for pleasure?

Fiction, primarily, plus the occasional biography or other subject. I do more and more rereading of my favourite books, as I'd hate to think I would never read any of them again. So that means I am no longer as adventurous a reader as I should be. Writers have to read as well as write, but I suppose if I have found what I think is the best, then it can't do any harm to my writing if I keep rereading it. I hope not, anyway!

What are your five favourite books, and why?
I have so many favourite books, but five which come immediately to mind are *Anna Karenina*, *Going to Meet the Man*, *Great Expectations*, *The House of Mirth* and *The Wine of Solitude*. I love classic Russian literature and, to my mind, no one can beat Tolstoy. His people are so real, I feel I know them. James Baldwin's *Going to Meet the Man* is a fabulous collection of short stories about Black experience from which I learned a lot. Dickens shares the humanity of these two authors, plus he's terribly funny. Edith Wharton's novels are superb and *The House of Mirth* is one of her most moving stories. I love anything by Irene Nemirovsky, so *The Wine of Solitude* has to stand for them all. And I'll cheat and add a sixth favourite, which really is a cheat because it comprises a series of seven novels: Gore Vidal's Narratives of Empire series exemplifies an entirely different approach to fiction that I find compelling and unsurpassed.

What is your e-reading device of choice?
Mine's an iPad. It's very adaptable for different formats and it also enables me to take photographs and videos, and record interviews, for my blog at Feed the Monkey.

Describe your desk
It's a big wooden dining table that we bought in France when we lived there for eight years. The table is far too big for our small house, but it would be such hard work getting it out the door that I think we're stuck with it. I just have my Mac computer on it, plus a coaster for my mug of tea or coffee, and my spectacles case. My wife, Brigitte, works on the other side of the table, so we share our thoughts and emails from time to time. Her presence helps me concentrate. Strangely enough, if I am on my own I spend far too much time staring out the window.

When you're not writing, how do you spend your time?
When I am not writing I am usually thinking about writing, or else promoting my writing. When I'm not doing any of those things I can usually be found reading books or watching films, which have always been my great passions in life. Brigitte and I have a gorgeous greyhound whom we adore and she takes up much of our time.

Questions for Reading Groups

1 What are the main problems that Stephen has to solve? Does he succeed?

2 Why do you think Stephen's important memories are recounted in the present tense?

3 In your opinion, how does the past affect the present in the novel?

4 What is your understanding of Stephen's indecision about what he should do?

5 Describe your response to the Hamlet imagery in the novel.

6 Describe Audrey's relationship with her children. What is positive, what negative?

7 How would you describe the women in the novel, especially Angela, Audrey and Lorna?

8 How is Giuliana separate from the other characters in the novel? What do you think of her?

9 In what ways does Stephen's university life cast light on his personal circumstances?

10 Discuss your interpretation of the ending of the novel. How does it make you feel?

CPSIA information can be obtained
at www.ICGtesting.com
Printed in the USA
LVHW010014210819
628406LV00007B/187/P